Henry James

Henry James OM (15 April 1843 – 28 February 1916) was an American-British author regarded as a key transitional figure between literary realism and literary modernism, and is considered by many to be among the greatest novelists in the English language. He was the son of Henry James Sr. and the brother of renowned philosopher and psychologist William James and diarist Alice James.

He is best known for a number of novels dealing with the social and marital interplay between émigré Americans, English people, and continental Europeans. Examples of such novels include The Portrait of a Lady, The Ambassadors, and The Wings of the Dove. His later works were increasingly experimental. In describing the internal states of mind and social dynamics of his characters, James often made use of a style in which ambiguous or contradictory motives and impressions were overlaid or juxtaposed in the discussion of a character's psyche.(Source: Wikipedia)

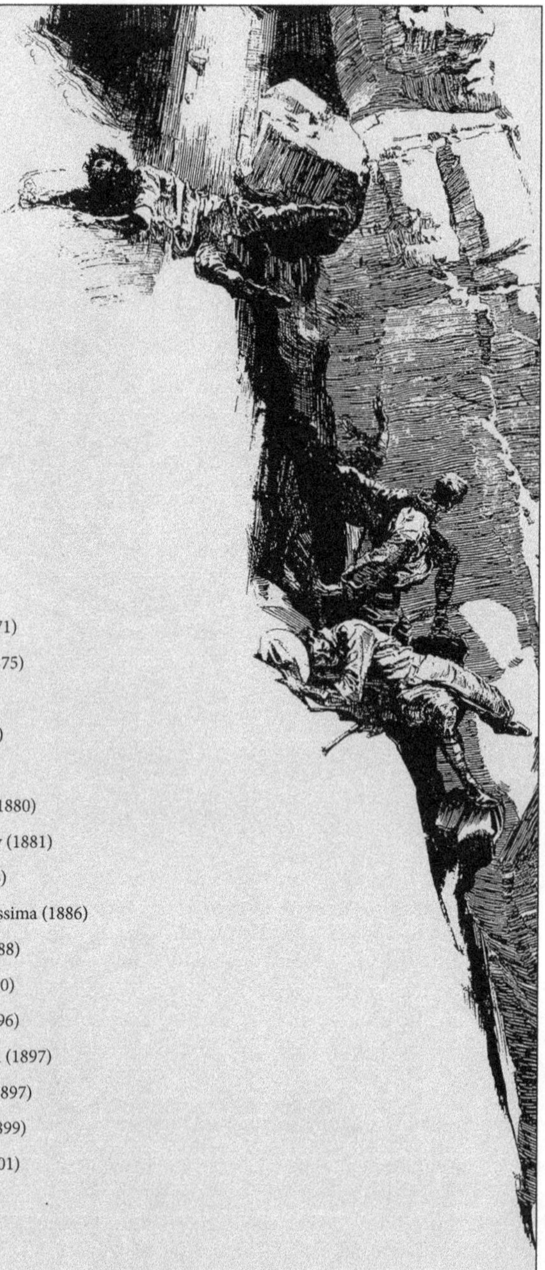

Literary works:

Watch and Ward (1871)

Roderick Hudson (1875)

The American (1877)

The Europeans (1878)

Confidence (1879)

Washington Square (1880)

The Portrait of a Lady (1881)

The Bostonians (1886)

The Princess Casamassima (1886)

The Reverberator (1888)

The Tragic Muse (1890)

The Other House (1896)

The Spoils of Poynton (1897)

What Maisie Knew (1897)

The Awkward Age (1899)

The Sacred Fount (1901)

THE WORKS OF HENRY JAMES

VOL. 17 (OF 36)

THE ASPERN PAPERS

THE AUTHOR OF BELTRAFFIO

An Imprint of Moon Classics LLC

A Wholly Owned Subsidiary of Queenior LLC

A Melodragon Company

First Printing: 2020

ISBN 978-1-6627-1580-8 (Paperback)

ISBN 978-1-6627-1581-5 (Hardcover)

Published by Moon Classics

www.moonclassics.com

Contents

THE

WORKS

OF

HENRY JAMES

VOL. 17 (OF 36)

THE ASPERN PAPERS

I

I had taken Mrs. Prest into my confidence; in truth without her I should have made but little advance, for the fruitful idea in the whole business dropped from her friendly lips. It was she who invented the short cut, who severed the Gordian knot. It is not supposed to be the nature of women to rise as a general thing to the largest and most liberal view—I mean of a practical scheme; but it has struck me that they sometimes throw off a bold conception—such as a man would not have risen to—with singular serenity. "Simply ask them to take you in on the footing of a lodger"—I don't think that unaided I should have risen to that. I was beating about the bush, trying to be ingenious, wondering by what combination of arts I might become an acquaintance, when she offered this happy suggestion that the way to become an acquaintance was first to become an inmate. Her actual knowledge of the Misses Bordereau was scarcely larger than mine, and indeed I had brought with me from England some definite facts which were new to her. Their name had been mixed up ages before with one of the greatest names of the century, and they lived now in Venice in obscurity, on very small means, unvisited, unapproachable, in a dilapidated old palace on an out-of-the-way canal: this was the substance of my friend's impression of them. She herself had been established in Venice for fifteen years and had done a great deal of good there; but the circle of her benevolence did not include the two shy, mysterious and, as it was somehow supposed, scarcely respectable Americans (they were believed to have lost in their long exile all national quality, besides having had, as their name implied, some French strain in their origin), who asked no favors and desired no attention. In the early years of her residence she had made an attempt to see them, but this had been successful only as regards the little one, as Mrs. Prest called the niece; though in reality as I afterward learned she was considerably the bigger of the two. She had heard Miss Bordereau was ill and had a suspicion that she was in want; and she had gone to the house to offer assistance, so that if there were suffering (and American suffering), she should at least not have it on her conscience. The "little one" received her in the great cold, tarnished Venetian sala, the central hall of the house, paved with marble and roofed with dim crossbeams, and did not even ask her to sit down. This was not encouraging for me, who wished to sit so fast, and I remarked as much to Mrs. Prest. She however replied with profundity, "Ah, but there's all the difference: I went to confer a favor and you will go to ask one. If they are proud you will be on the right side." And she offered to show me their house to begin with—to row me thither in her gondola. I let her know that I had already been to look at it half a dozen times; but I accepted her invitation, for it charmed me to hover about the place. I had made my way to it the day after my arrival in Venice (it had been described to me in advance by the friend in England to whom I owed definite information as to their possession of the papers), and I had besieged it with my eyes while I considered my plan of campaign. Jeffrey Aspern had never been in it that I knew of; but some note of his voice seemed to abide there by a roundabout implication, a faint reverberation.

Mrs. Prest knew nothing about the papers, but she was interested in my curiosity, as she was always interested in the joys and sorrows of her friends. As we went, however, in her gondola, gliding there under the sociable hood with the bright Venetian picture framed on either side by the movable window, I could see that she was amused by my infatuation, the way my interest in the papers had become a fixed idea. "One would think you expected to find in them the answer to the riddle of the universe," she said; and I denied the impeachment only by replying that if I had to choose between that precious solution and a bundle of Jeffrey Aspern's letters I knew indeed which would appear to me the greater boon. She pretended to make light of his genius, and I took no pains to defend him. One doesn't defend one's god: one's god is in himself a defense. Besides, today, after his long comparative obscuration, he hangs high in the heaven of our literature, for all the world to see; he is a part of the light by which we walk. The most I said was that he was no doubt not a woman's poet: to which she rejoined aptly enough that he had been at least Miss Bordereau's. The strange thing had been for me to discover in England that she was still alive: it was as if I had been told Mrs. Siddons was, or Queen Caroline, or the famous Lady Hamilton, for it seemed to me that she belonged to a generation as extinct. "Why, she must be tremendously old—at least a hundred," I had said; but on coming to consider dates I saw that it was not strictly necessary that she should have exceeded by very much the common span. Nonetheless she was very far advanced in life, and her relations with Jeffrey Aspern had occurred in her early womanhood. "That is her excuse," said Mrs. Prest, half-sententiously and yet also somewhat as if she were ashamed of making a speech so little in the real tone of Venice. As if a woman needed an excuse for having loved the divine poet! He had been not only one of the most brilliant minds of his day (and in those years, when the century was young, there were, as everyone knows, many), but one of the most genial men and one of the handsomest.

The niece, according to Mrs. Prest, was not so old, and she risked the conjecture that she was only a grandniece. This was possible; I had nothing but my share in the very limited knowledge of my English fellow worshipper John Cumnor, who had never seen the couple. The world, as I say, had recognized Jeffrey Aspern, but Cumnor and I had recognized him most. The multitude, today, flocked to his temple, but of that temple he and I regarded ourselves as the ministers. We held, justly, as I think, that we had done more for his memory than anyone else, and we had done it by opening lights into his life. He had nothing to fear from us because he had nothing to fear from the truth, which alone at such a distance of time we could be interested in establishing. His early death had been the only dark spot in his life, unless the papers in Miss Bordereau's hands should perversely bring out others. There had been an impression about 1825 that he had "treated her badly," just as there had been an impression that he had "served," as the London populace says, several other ladies in the same way. Each of these cases Cumnor and I had been able to investigate, and we had never failed to acquit him conscientiously of shabby behavior. I judged him perhaps more indulgently than my friend; certainly, at any rate, it appeared to me that no man could have walked straighter in the given circumstances. These were almost always awkward. Half the women of his time, to speak liberally, had flung themselves at his head, and out of this pernicious fashion many complications, some of them grave, had not failed to arise. He was not a woman's poet, as I had said to Mrs. Prest, in the modern phase of his reputation; but the situation had been different when the man's own voice was mingled with his song. That voice, by every testimony, was one of the sweetest ever heard. "Orpheus and the Maenads!" was the exclamation that rose to my lips when I first turned over his correspondence. Almost all the Maenads were unreasonable, and many of them insupportable; it struck me in short that he was kinder, more considerate than, in his place (if I could imagine myself in such a place!) I should have been.

It was certainly strange beyond all strangeness, and I shall not take up space with attempting to explain it, that whereas in all these other lines of research we had to deal with phantoms and dust, the mere echoes of echoes, the one living source of information that had lingered on into our time had been unheeded by us. Every one of Aspern's contemporaries had, according to our belief, passed away; we had not been able to look into a single pair of eyes into which his had looked or to feel a transmitted contact in any aged hand that his had touched. Most dead of all did poor Miss Bordereau appear, and yet she alone had survived. We exhausted in the course of months our wonder that we had not found her out sooner, and the substance of our explanation was that she had kept so quiet. The poor lady on the whole had had reason for doing so. But it was a revelation to us that it was possible to keep so quiet as that in the latter half of the nineteenth century—the age of newspapers and telegrams and photographs and interviewers. And she had taken no great trouble about it either: she had not hidden herself away in an undiscoverable hole; she had boldly settled down in a city of exhibition. The only secret of her safety that we could perceive was that Venice contained so many curiosities that were greater than she. And then accident had somehow favored her, as was shown for example in the fact that Mrs. Prest had never happened to mention her to me, though I had spent three weeks in Venice—under her nose, as it were—five years before. Mrs. Prest had not mentioned this much to anyone; she appeared almost to have forgotten she was there. Of course she had not the responsibilities of an editor. It was no explanation of the old woman's having eluded us to say that she lived abroad, for our researches had again and again taken us (not only by correspondence but by personal inquiry) to France, to Germany, to Italy, in which countries, not counting his important stay in England, so many of the too few years of Aspern's career were spent. We were glad to think at least that in all our publishings (some people consider I believe that we have overdone them), we had only touched in passing and in the most discreet manner on Miss Bordereau's connection. Oddly enough, even if we had had the material (and we often wondered what had become of it), it would have been the most difficult episode to handle.

The gondola stopped, the old palace was there; it was a house of the class which in Venice carries even in extreme dilapidation the dignified name. "How charming! It's gray and pink!" my companion exclaimed; and that is the most comprehensive description of it. It was not particularly old, only two or three centuries; and it had an air not so much of decay as of quiet discouragement, as if it had rather missed its career. But its wide front, with a stone balcony from end to end of the piano nobile or most important floor, was architectural enough, with the aid of various pilasters and arches; and the stucco with which in the intervals it had long ago been endued was rosy in the April afternoon. It overlooked a clean, melancholy, unfrequented canal, which had a narrow riva or convenient footway on either side. "I don't know why—there are no brick gables," said Mrs. Prest, "but this corner has seemed to me before more Dutch than Italian, more like Amsterdam than like Venice. It's perversely clean, for reasons of its own; and though you can pass on foot scarcely anyone ever thinks of doing so. It has the air of a Protestant Sunday. Perhaps the people are afraid of the Misses Bordereau. I daresay they have the reputation of witches."

I forget what answer I made to this—I was given up to two other reflections. The first of these was that if the old lady lived in such a big, imposing house she could not be in any sort of misery and therefore would not be tempted by a chance to let a couple of rooms. I expressed this idea to Mrs. Prest, who gave me a very logical reply. "If she didn't live in a big house how could it be a question of her having rooms to spare? If she were not amply lodged herself you would lack ground to approach her. Besides, a big house here, and especially in this quartier perdu, proves nothing at all: it is perfectly compatible with a state of penury. Dilapidated old palazzi, if you will go out of the way for them, are to be had for five shillings a year. And as for the people who live in them—no, until you have explored Venice socially as much as I have you can form no idea of their domestic desolation. They live on nothing, for they have nothing to live on." The other idea that had come into my head was connected with a high blank wall which appeared to confine an expanse of ground on one side of the house. Blank I call it, but it was figured over with the patches that please a painter, repaired breaches, crumblings of plaster, extrusions of brick that had turned pink with time; and a few thin trees, with the poles of certain rickety trellises, were visible over the top. The place was a garden, and apparently it belonged to the house. It suddenly occurred to me that if it did belong to the house I had my pretext.

I sat looking out on all this with Mrs. Prest (it was covered with the golden glow of Venice) from the shade of our felze, and she asked me if I would go in then, while she waited for me, or come back another time. At first I could not decide—it was doubtless very weak of me. I wanted still to think I MIGHT get a footing, and I was afraid to meet failure, for it would leave me, as I remarked to my companion, without another arrow for my bow. "Why not another?" she inquired as I sat there hesitating and thinking it over; and she wished to know why even now and before taking the trouble of becoming an inmate (which might be wretchedly uncomfortable after all, even if it succeeded), I had not the resource of simply offering them a sum of money down. In that way I might obtain the documents without bad nights.

"Dearest lady," I exclaimed, "excuse the impatience of my tone when I suggest that you must have forgotten the very fact (surely I communicated it to you) which pushed me to throw myself upon your ingenuity. The old woman won't have the documents spoken of; they are personal, delicate, intimate, and she hasn't modern notions, God bless her! If I should sound that note first I should certainly spoil the game. I can arrive at the papers only by putting her off her guard, and I can put her off her guard only by ingratiating diplomatic practices. Hypocrisy, duplicity are my only chance. I am sorry for it, but for Jeffrey Aspern's sake I would do worse still. First I must take tea with her; then tackle the main job." And I told over what had happened to John Cumnor when he wrote to her. No notice whatever had been taken of his first letter, and the second had been answered very sharply, in six lines, by the niece. "Miss Bordereau requested her to say that she could not imagine what he meant by troubling them. They had none of Mr. Aspern's papers, and if they had should never think of showing them to anyone on any account whatever. She didn't know what he was talking about and begged he would let her alone." I certainly did not want to be met that way.

"Well," said Mrs. Prest after a moment, provokingly, "perhaps after all they haven't any of his things. If they deny it flat how are you sure?"

"John Cumnor is sure, and it would take me long to tell you how his conviction, or his very strong presumption—strong enough to stand against the old lady's not unnatural fib—has built itself up. Besides, he makes much of the internal evidence of the niece's letter."

"The internal evidence?"

"Her calling him 'Mr. Aspern.'"

"I don't see what that proves."

"It proves familiarity, and familiarity implies the possession of mementoes, or relics. I can't tell you how that 'Mr.' touches me—how it bridges over the gulf of time and brings our hero near to me—nor what an edge it gives to my desire to see Juliana. You don't say, 'Mr.' Shakespeare."

"Would I, any more, if I had a box full of his letters?"

"Yes, if he had been your lover and someone wanted them!" And I added that John Cumnor was so convinced, and so all the more convinced by Miss Bordereau's tone, that he would have come himself to Venice on the business were it not that for him there was the obstacle that it would be difficult to disprove his identity with the person who had written to them, which the old ladies would be sure to suspect in spite of dissimulation and a change of name. If they were to ask him point-blank if he were not their correspondent it would be too awkward for him to lie; whereas I was fortunately not tied in that way. I was a fresh hand and could say no without lying.

"But you will have to change your name," said Mrs. Prest. "Juliana lives out of the world as much as it is possible to live, but none the less she has probably heard of Mr. Aspern's editors; she perhaps possesses what you have published."

"I have thought of that," I returned; and I drew out of my pocketbook a visiting card, neatly engraved with a name that was not my own.

"You are very extravagant; you might have written it," said my companion.

"This looks more genuine."

"Certainly, you are prepared to go far! But it will be awkward about your letters; they won't come to you in that mask."

"My banker will take them in, and I will go every day to fetch them. It will give me a little walk."

"Shall you only depend upon that?" asked Mrs. Prest. "Aren't you coming to see me?"

"Oh, you will have left Venice, for the hot months, long before there are any results. I am prepared to roast all summer—as well as hereafter, perhaps you'll say! Meanwhile, John Cumnor will bombard me with letters addressed, in my feigned name, to the care of the padrona."

"She will recognize his hand," my companion suggested.

"On the envelope he can disguise it."

"Well, you're a precious pair! Doesn't it occur to you that even if you are able to say you are not Mr. Cumnor in person they may still suspect you of being his emissary?"

"Certainly, and I see only one way to parry that."

"And what may that be?"

I hesitated a moment. "To make love to the niece."

"Ah," cried Mrs. Prest, "wait till you see her!

II

"I must work the garden—I must work the garden," I said to myself, five minutes later, as I waited, upstairs, in the long, dusky sala, where the bare scagliola floor gleamed vaguely in a chink of the closed shutters. The place was impressive but it looked cold and cautious. Mrs. Prest had floated away, giving me a rendezvous at the end of half an hour by some neighboring water steps; and I had been let into the house, after pulling the rusty bell wire, by a little red-headed, white-faced maidservant, who was very young and not ugly and wore clicking pattens and a shawl in the fashion of a hood. She had not contented herself with opening the door from above by the usual arrangement of a creaking pulley, though she had looked down at me first from an upper window, dropping the inevitable challenge which in Italy precedes the hospitable act. As a general thing I was irritated by this survival of medieval manners, though as I liked the old I suppose I ought to have liked it; but I was so determined to be genial that I took my false card out of my pocket and held it up to her, smiling as if it were a magic token. It had the effect of one indeed, for it brought her, as I say, all the way down. I begged her to hand it to her mistress, having first written on it in Italian the words, "Could you very kindly see a gentleman, an American, for a moment?" The little maid was not hostile, and I reflected that even that was perhaps something gained. She colored, she smiled and looked both frightened and pleased. I could see that my arrival was a great affair, that visits were rare in that house, and that she was a person who would have liked a sociable place. When she pushed forward the heavy door behind me I felt that I had a foot in the citadel. She pattered across the damp, stony lower hall and I followed her up the high staircase—stonier still, as it seemed—without an invitation. I think she had meant I should wait for her below, but such was not my idea, and I took up my station in the sala. She flitted, at the far end of it, into impenetrable regions, and I looked at the place with my heart beating as I had known it to do in the dentist's parlor. It was gloomy and stately, but it owed its character almost entirely to its noble shape and to the fine architectural doors—as high as the doors of houses—which, leading into the various rooms, repeated themselves on either side at intervals. They were surmounted with old faded painted escutcheons, and here and there, in the spaces between them, brown pictures, which I perceived to be bad, in battered frames, were suspended. With the exception of several straw-bottomed chairs with their backs to the wall, the grand obscure vista contained nothing else to minister to effect. It was evidently never used save as a passage, and little even as that. I may add that by the time the door opened again through which the maidservant had escaped, my eyes had grown used to the want of light.

I had not meant by my private ejaculation that I must myself cultivate the soil of the tangled enclosure which lay beneath the windows, but the lady who came toward me from the distance over the hard, shining floor might have supposed as much from the way in which, as I went rapidly to meet her, I exclaimed, taking care to speak Italian: "The garden, the garden—do me the pleasure to tell me if it's yours!"

She stopped short, looking at me with wonder; and then, "Nothing here is mine," she answered in English, coldly and sadly.

"Oh, you are English; how delightful!" I remarked, ingenuously. "But surely the garden belongs to the house?"

"Yes, but the house doesn't belong to me." She was a long, lean, pale person, habited apparently in a dull-colored dressing gown, and she spoke with a kind of mild literalness. She did not ask me to sit down, any more than years before (if she were the niece) she had asked Mrs. Prest, and we stood face to face in the empty pompous hall.

"Well then, would you kindly tell me to whom I must address myself? I'm afraid you'll think me odiously intrusive, but you know I MUST have a garden—upon my honor I must!"

Her face was not young, but it was simple; it was not fresh, but it was mild. She had large eyes which were not bright, and a great deal of hair which was not "dressed," and long fine hands which were—possibly—not clean. She clasped these members almost convulsively as, with a confused, alarmed look, she broke out, "Oh, don't take it away from us; we like it ourselves!"

"You have the use of it then?"

"Oh, yes. If it wasn't for that!" And she gave a shy, melancholy smile.

"Isn't it a luxury, precisely? That's why, intending to be in Venice some weeks, possibly all summer, and having some literary work, some reading and writing to do, so that I must be quiet, and yet if possible a great deal in the open air—that's why I have felt that a garden is really indispensable. I appeal to your own experience," I went on, smiling. "Now can't I look at yours?"

"I don't know, I don't understand," the poor woman murmured, planted there and letting her embarrassed eyes wander all over my strangeness.

"I mean only from one of those windows—such grand ones as you have here—if you will let me open the shutters." And I walked toward the back of the house. When I had advanced halfway I stopped and waited, as if I took it for granted she would accompany me. I had been of necessity very abrupt, but I strove at the same time to give her the impression of extreme courtesy. "I have been looking at furnished rooms all over the place, and it seems impossible to find any with a garden attached. Naturally in a place like Venice gardens are rare. It's absurd if you like, for a man, but I can't live without flowers."

"There are none to speak of down there." She came nearer to me, as if, though she mistrusted me, I had drawn her by an invisible thread. I went on again, and she continued as she followed me: "We have a few, but they are very common. It costs too much to cultivate them; one has to have a man."

"Why shouldn't I be the man?" I asked. "I'll work without wages; or rather I'll put in a gardener. You shall have the sweetest flowers in Venice."

She protested at this, with a queer little sigh which might also have been a gush of rapture at the picture I presented. Then she observed, "We don't know you—we don't know you."

"You know me as much as I know you: that is much more, because you know my name. And if you are English I am almost a countryman."

"We are not English," said my companion, watching me helplessly while I threw open the shutters of one of the divisions of the wide high window.

"You speak the language so beautifully: might I ask what you are?" Seen from above the garden was certainly shabby; but I perceived at a glance that it had great capabilities. She made no rejoinder, she was so lost in staring at me, and I exclaimed, "You don't mean to say you are also by chance American?"

"I don't know; we used to be."

"Used to be? Surely you haven't changed?"

"It's so many years ago—we are nothing."

"So many years that you have been living here? Well, I don't wonder at that; it's a grand old house. I suppose you all use the garden," I went on, "but I assure you I shouldn't be in your way. I would be very quiet and stay in one corner."

"We all use it?" she repeated after me, vaguely, not coming close to the window but looking at my shoes. She appeared to think me capable of throwing her out.

"I mean all your family, as many as you are."

"There is only one other; she is very old—she never goes down."

"Only one other, in all this great house!" I feigned to be not only amazed but almost scandalized. "Dear lady, you must have space then to spare!"

"To spare?" she repeated, in the same dazed way.

"Why, you surely don't live (two quiet women—I see YOU are quiet, at any rate) in fifty rooms!" Then with a burst of hope and cheer I demanded: "Couldn't you let me two or three? That would set me up!"

I had not struck the note that translated my purpose, and I need not reproduce the whole of the tune I played. I ended by making my interlocutress believe that I was an honorable person, though of course I did not even attempt to persuade her that I was not an eccentric one. I repeated that I had studies to pursue; that I wanted quiet; that I delighted in a garden and had vainly sought one up and down the city; that I would undertake that before another month was over the dear old house should be smothered in flowers.

I think it was the flowers that won my suit, for I afterward found that Miss Tita (for such the name of this high tremulous spinster proved somewhat incongruously to be) had an insatiable appetite for them. When I speak of my suit as won I mean that before I left her she had promised that she would refer the question to her aunt. I inquired who her aunt might be and she answered, "Why, Miss Bordereau!" with an air of surprise, as if I might have been expected to know. There were contradictions like this in Tita Bordereau which, as I observed later, contributed to make her an odd and affecting person. It was the study of the two ladies to live so that the world should not touch them, and yet they had never altogether accepted the idea that it never heard of them. In Tita at any rate a grateful susceptibility to human contact had not died out, and contact of a limited order there would be if I should come to live in the house.

"We have never done anything of the sort; we have never had a lodger or any kind of inmate." So much as this she made a point of saying to me. "We are very poor, we live very badly. The rooms are very bare—that you might take; they have nothing in them. I don't know how you would sleep, how you would eat."

"With your permission, I could easily put in a bed and a few tables and chairs. C'est la moindre des choses and the affair of an hour or two. I know a little man from whom I can hire what I should want for a few months, for a trifle, and my gondolier can bring the things round in his boat. Of course in this great house you must have a second kitchen, and my servant, who is a wonderfully handy fellow" (this personage was an evocation of the moment), "can easily cook me a chop there. My tastes and habits are of the simplest; I live on flowers!" And then I ventured to add that if they were very poor it was all the more reason they should let their rooms. They were bad economists—I had never heard of such a waste of material.

I saw in a moment that the good lady had never before been spoken to in that way, with a kind of humorous firmness which did not exclude sympathy but was on the contrary founded on it. She might easily have told me that my sympathy was impertinent, but this by good fortune did not occur to her. I left her with the understanding that she would consider the matter with her aunt and that I might come back the next day for their decision.

"The aunt will refuse; she will think the whole proceeding very louche!" Mrs. Prest declared shortly after this, when I had resumed my place in her gondola. She had put the idea into my head and now (so little are women to be counted on) she appeared to take a despondent view of it. Her pessimism provoked me and I pretended to have the best hopes; I went so far as to say that I had a distinct presentiment that I should succeed. Upon this Mrs. Prest broke out, "Oh, I see what's in your head! You fancy you have made such an impression in a quarter of an hour that she is dying for you to come and can be depended upon to bring the old one round. If you do get in you'll count it as a triumph."

I did count it as a triumph, but only for the editor (in the last analysis), not for the man, who had not the tradition of personal conquest. When I went back on the morrow the little maidservant conducted me straight through the long sala (it opened there as before in perfect perspective and was lighter now, which I thought a good omen) into the apartment from which the recipient of my former visit had emerged on that occasion. It was a large shabby parlor, with a fine old painted ceiling and a strange figure sitting alone at one of the windows. They come back to me now almost with the palpitation they caused, the successive feelings that accompanied my consciousness that as the door of the room closed behind me I was really face to face with the Juliana of some of Aspern's most exquisite and most renowned lyrics. I grew used to her afterward, though never completely; but as she sat there before me my heart beat as fast as if the miracle of resurrection had taken place for my benefit. Her presence seemed somehow to contain his, and I felt nearer to him at that first moment of seeing her than I ever had been before or ever have been since. Yes, I remember my emotions in their order, even including a curious little tremor that took me when I saw that the niece was not there. With her, the day before, I had become sufficiently familiar, but it almost exceeded my courage (much as I had longed for the event) to be left alone with such a terrible relic as the aunt. She was too strange, too literally resurgent. Then came a check, with the perception that we were not really face to face, inasmuch as she had over her eyes a horrible green shade which, for her, served almost as a mask. I believed for the instant that she had put it on expressly, so that from underneath it she might scrutinize me without being scrutinized herself. At the same time it increased the presumption that there was a ghastly death's-head lurking behind it. The divine Juliana as a grinning skull—the vision hung there until it passed. Then it came to me that she WAS tremendously old—so old that death might take her at any moment, before I had time to get what I wanted from her. The next thought was a correction to that; it lighted up the situation. She would die next week, she would die tomorrow—then I could seize her papers. Meanwhile she sat there neither moving nor speaking. She was very small and shrunken, bent forward, with her hands in her lap. She was dressed in black, and her head was wrapped in a piece of old black lace which showed no hair.

My emotion keeping me silent she spoke first, and the remark she made was exactly the most unexpected.

III

"Our house is very far from the center, but the little canal is very comme il faut."

"It's the sweetest corner of Venice and I can imagine nothing more charming," I hastened to reply. The old lady's voice was very thin and weak, but it had an agreeable, cultivated murmur, and there was wonder in the thought that that individual note had been in Jeffrey Aspern's ear.

"Please to sit down there. I hear very well," she said quietly, as if perhaps I had been shouting at her; and the chair she pointed to was at a certain distance. I took possession of it, telling her that I was perfectly aware that I had intruded, that I had not been properly introduced and could only throw myself upon her indulgence. Perhaps the other lady, the one I had had the honor of seeing the day before, would have explained to her about the garden. That was literally what had given me courage to take a step so unconventional. I had fallen in love at sight with the whole place (she herself probably was so used to it that she did not know the impression it was capable of making on a stranger), and I had felt it was really a case to risk something. Was her own kindness in receiving me a sign that I was not wholly out in my calculation? It would render me extremely happy to think so. I could give her my word of honor that I was a most respectable, inoffensive person and that as an inmate they would be barely conscious of my existence. I would conform to any regulations, any restrictions if they would only let me enjoy the garden. Moreover I should be delighted to give her references, guarantees; they would be of the very best, both in Venice and in England as well as in America.

She listened to me in perfect stillness and I felt that she was looking at me with great attention, though I could see only the lower part of her bleached and shriveled face. Independently of the refining process of old age it had a delicacy which once must have been great. She had been very fair, she had had a wonderful complexion. She was silent a little after I had ceased speaking; then she inquired, "If you are so fond of a garden why don't you go to terra firma, where there are so many far better than this?"

"Oh, it's the combination!" I answered, smiling; and then, with rather a flight of fancy, "It's the idea of a garden in the middle of the sea."

"It's not in the middle of the sea; you can't see the water."

I stared a moment, wondering whether she wished to convict me of fraud. "Can't see the water? Why, dear madam, I can come up to the very gate in my boat."

She appeared inconsequent, for she said vaguely in reply to this, "Yes, if you have got a boat. I haven't any; it's many years since I have been in one of the gondolas." She uttered these words as if the gondolas were a curious faraway craft which she knew only by hearsay.

"Let me assure you of the pleasure with which I would put mine at your service!" I exclaimed. I had scarcely said this, however, before I became aware that the speech was in questionable taste and might also do me the injury of making me appear too eager, too possessed of a hidden motive. But the old woman remained impenetrable and her attitude bothered me by suggesting that she had a fuller vision of me than I had of her. She gave me no thanks for my somewhat extravagant offer but remarked that the lady I had seen the day before was her niece; she would presently come in. She had asked her to stay away a little on purpose, because she herself wished to see me at first alone. She relapsed into silence, and I asked myself why she had judged this necessary and what was coming yet; also whether I might venture on some judicious remark in praise of her companion. I went so far as to say that I should be delighted to see her again: she had been so very courteous to me, considering how odd she must have thought me—a declaration which drew from Miss Bordereau another of her whimsical speeches.

"She has very good manners; I bred her up myself!" I was on the point of saying that that accounted for the easy grace of the niece, but I arrested myself in time, and the next moment the old woman went on: "I don't care who you may be—I don't want to know; it signifies very little today." This had all the air of being a formula of dismissal, as if her next words would be that I might take myself off now that she had had the amusement of looking on the face of such a monster of indiscretion. Therefore I was all the more surprised when she added, with her soft, venerable quaver, "You may have as many rooms as you like—if you will pay a good deal of money."

I hesitated but for a single instant, long enough to ask myself what she meant in particular by this condition. First it struck me that she must have really a large sum in her mind; then I reasoned quickly that her idea of a large sum would probably not correspond to my own. My deliberation, I think, was not so visible as to diminish the promptitude with which I replied, "I will pay with pleasure and of course in advance whatever you may think is proper to ask me."

"Well then, a thousand francs a month," she rejoined instantly, while her baffling green shade continued to cover her attitude.

The figure, as they say, was startling and my logic had been at fault. The sum she had mentioned was, by the Venetian measure of such matters, exceedingly large; there was many an old palace in an out-of-the-way corner that I might on such terms have enjoyed by the year. But so far as my small means allowed I was prepared to spend money, and my decision was quickly taken. I would pay her with a smiling face what she asked, but in that case I would give myself the compensation of extracting the papers from her for nothing. Moreover if she had asked five times as much I should have risen to the occasion; so odious would it have appeared to me to stand chaffering with Aspern's Juliana. It was queer enough to have a question of money with her at all. I assured her that her views perfectly met my own and that on the morrow I should have the pleasure of putting three months' rent into her hand. She received this announcement with serenity and with no apparent sense that after all it would be becoming of her to say that I ought to see the rooms first. This did not occur to her and indeed her serenity was mainly what I wanted. Our little bargain was just concluded when the door opened and the younger lady appeared on the threshold. As soon as Miss Bordereau saw her niece she cried out almost gaily, "He will give three thousand—three thousand tomorrow!"

Miss Tita stood still, with her patient eyes turning from one of us to the other; then she inquired, scarcely above her breath, "Do you mean francs?"

"Did you mean francs or dollars?" the old woman asked of me at this.

"I think francs were what you said," I answered, smiling.

"That is very good," said Miss Tita, as if she had become conscious that her own question might have looked overreaching.

"What do YOU know? You are ignorant," Miss Bordereau remarked; not with acerbity but with a strange, soft coldness.

"Yes, of money—certainly of money!" Miss Tita hastened to exclaim.

"I am sure you have your own branches of knowledge," I took the liberty of saying, genially. There was something painful to me, somehow, in the turn the conversation had taken, in the discussion of the rent.

"She had a very good education when she was young. I looked into that myself," said Miss Bordereau. Then she added, "But she has learned nothing since."

"I have always been with you," Miss Tita rejoined very mildly, and evidently with no intention of making an epigram.

"Yes, but for that!" her aunt declared with more satirical force. She evidently meant that but for this her niece would never have got on at all; the point of the observation however being lost on Miss Tita, though she blushed at hearing her history revealed to a stranger. Miss Bordereau went on, addressing herself to me: "And what time will you come tomorrow with the money?"

"The sooner the better. If it suits you I will come at noon."

"I am always here but I have my hours," said the old woman, as if her convenience were not to be taken for granted.

"You mean the times when you receive?"

"I never receive. But I will see you at noon, when you come with the money."

"Very good, I shall be punctual;" and I added, "May I shake hands with you, on our contract?" I thought there ought to be some little form, it would make me really feel easier, for I foresaw that there would be no other. Besides, though Miss Bordereau could not today be called personally attractive and there was something even in her wasted antiquity that bade one stand at one's distance, I felt an irresistible desire to hold in my own for a moment the hand that Jeffrey Aspern had pressed.

For a minute she made no answer, and I saw that my proposal failed to meet with her approbation. She indulged in no movement of withdrawal, which I half-expected; she only said coldly, "I belong to a time when that was not the custom."

I felt rather snubbed but I exclaimed good humoredly to Miss Tita, "Oh, you will do as well!" I shook hands with her while she replied, with a small flutter, "Yes, yes, to show it's all arranged!"

"Shall you bring the money in gold?" Miss Bordereau demanded, as I was turning to the door.

I looked at her for a moment. "Aren't you a little afraid, after all, of keeping such a sum as that in the house?" It was not that I was annoyed at her avidity but I was really struck with the disparity between such a treasure and such scanty means of guarding it.

"Whom should I be afraid of if I am not afraid of you?" she asked with her shrunken grimness.

"Ah well," said I, laughing, "I shall be in point of fact a protector and I will bring gold if you prefer."

"Thank you," the old woman returned with dignity and with an inclination of her head which evidently signified that I might depart. I passed out of the room, reflecting that it would not be easy to circumvent her. As I stood in the sala again I saw that Miss Tita had followed me, and I supposed that as her aunt had neglected to suggest that I should take a look at my quarters it was her purpose to repair the omission. But she made no such suggestion; she only stood there with a dim, though not a languid smile, and with an effect of irresponsible, incompetent youth which was almost comically at variance with the faded facts of her person. She was not infirm, like her aunt, but she struck me as still more helpless, because her inefficiency was spiritual, which was not the case with Miss Bordereau's. I waited to see if she would offer to show me the rest of the house, but I did not precipitate the question, inasmuch as my plan was from this moment to spend as much of my time as possible in her society. I only observed at the end of a minute:

"I have had better fortune than I hoped. It was very kind of her to see me. Perhaps you said a good word for me."

"It was the idea of the money," said Miss Tita.

"And did you suggest that?"

"I told her that you would perhaps give a good deal."

"What made you think that?"

"I told her I thought you were rich."

"And what put that idea into your head?"

"I don't know; the way you talked."

"Dear me, I must talk differently now," I declared. "I'm sorry to say it's not the case."

"Well," said Miss Tita, "I think that in Venice the forestieri, in general, often give a great deal for something that after all isn't much." She appeared to make this remark with a comforting intention, to wish to remind me that if I had been extravagant I was not really foolishly singular. We walked together along the sala, and as I took its magnificent measure I said to her that I was afraid it would not form a part of my quartiere. Were my rooms by chance to be among those that opened into it? "Not if you go above, on the second floor," she answered with a little startled air, as if she had rather taken for granted I would know my proper place.

"And I infer that that's where your aunt would like me to be."

"She said your apartments ought to be very distinct."

"That certainly would be best." And I listened with respect while she told me that up above I was free to take whatever I liked; that there was another staircase, but only from the floor on which we stood, and that to pass from it to the garden-story or to come up to my lodging I should have in effect to cross the great hall. This was an immense point gained; I foresaw that it would constitute my whole leverage in my relations with the two ladies. When I asked Miss Tita how I was to manage at present to find my way up she replied with an access of that sociable shyness which constantly marked her manner.

"Perhaps you can't. I don't see—unless I should go with you." She evidently had not thought of this before.

We ascended to the upper floor and visited a long succession of empty rooms. The best of them looked over the garden; some of the others had a view of the blue lagoon, above the opposite rough-tiled housetops. They were all dusty and even a little disfigured with long neglect, but I saw that by spending a few hundred francs I should be able to convert three or four of them into a convenient habitation. My experiment was turning out costly, yet now that I had all but taken possession I ceased to allow this to trouble me. I mentioned to my companion a few of the things that I should put in, but she replied rather more precipitately than usual that I might do exactly what I liked; she seemed to wish to notify me that the Misses Bordereau would take no overt interest in my proceedings. I guessed that her aunt had instructed her to adopt this tone, and I may as well say now that I came afterward to distinguish perfectly (as I believed) between the speeches she made on her own responsibility and those the old lady imposed upon her. She took no notice of the unswept condition of the rooms and indulged in no explanations nor apologies. I said to myself that this was a sign that Juliana and her niece (disenchanting idea!) were untidy persons, with a low Italian standard; but I afterward recognized that a lodger who had forced an entrance had no locus standi as a critic. We looked out of a good many windows, for there was nothing within the rooms to look at, and still I wanted to linger. I asked her what several different objects in the prospect might be, but in no case did she appear to know. She was evidently not familiar with the view—it was as if she had not looked at it for years—and I presently saw that she was too preoccupied with something else to pretend to care for it. Suddenly she said—the remark was not suggested:

"I don't know whether it will make any difference to you, but the money is for me."

"The money?"

"The money you are going to bring."

"Why, you'll make me wish to stay here two or three years." I spoke as benevolently as possible, though it had begun to act on my nerves that with these women so associated with Aspern the pecuniary question should constantly come back.

"That would be very good for me," she replied, smiling.

"You put me on my honor!"

She looked as if she failed to understand this, but went on: "She wants me to have more. She thinks she is going to die."

"Ah, not soon, I hope!" I exclaimed with genuine feeling. I had perfectly considered the possibility that she would destroy her papers on the day she should feel her end really approach. I believed that she would cling to them till then, and I think I had an idea that she read Aspern's letters over every night or at least pressed them to her withered lips. I would have given a good deal to have a glimpse of the latter spectacle. I asked Miss Tita if the old lady were seriously ill, and she replied that she was only very tired—she had lived so very, very long. That was what she said herself—she wanted to die for a change. Besides, all her friends were dead long ago; either they ought to have remained or she ought to have gone. That was another thing her aunt often said—she was not at all content.

"But people don't die when they like, do they?" Miss Tita inquired. I took the liberty of asking why, if there was actually enough money to maintain both of them, there would not be more than enough in case of her being left alone. She considered this difficult problem a moment and then she said, "Oh, well, you know, she takes care of me. She thinks that when I'm alone I shall be a great fool, I shall not know how to manage."

"I should have supposed that you took care of her. I'm afraid she is very proud."

"Why, have you discovered that already?" Miss Tita cried with the glimmer of an illumination in her face.

"I was shut up with her there for a considerable time, and she struck me, she interested me extremely. It didn't take me long to make my discovery. She won't have much to say to me while I'm here."

"No, I don't think she will," my companion averred.

"Do you suppose she has some suspicion of me?"

Miss Tita's honest eyes gave me no sign that I had touched a mark. "I shouldn't think so—letting you in after all so easily."

"Oh, so easily! she has covered her risk. But where is it that one could take an advantage of her?"

"I oughtn't to tell you if I knew, ought I?" And Miss Tita added, before I had time to reply to this, smiling dolefully, "Do you think we have any weak points?"

"That's exactly what I'm asking. You would only have to mention them for me to respect them religiously."

She looked at me, at this, with that air of timid but candid and even gratified curiosity with which she had confronted me from the first; and then she said, "There is nothing to tell. We are terribly quiet. I don't know how the days pass. We have no life."

"I wish I might think that I should bring you a little."

"Oh, we know what we want," she went on. "It's all right."

There were various things I desired to ask her: how in the world they did live; whether they had any friends or visitors, any relations in America or in other countries. But I judged such an inquiry would be premature; I must leave it to a later chance. "Well, don't YOU be proud," I contented myself with saying. "Don't hide from me altogether."

"Oh, I must stay with my aunt," she returned, without looking at me. And at the same moment, abruptly, without any ceremony of parting, she quitted me and disappeared, leaving me to make my own way downstairs. I remained a while longer, wandering about the bright desert (the sun was pouring in) of the old house, thinking the situation over on the spot. Not even the pattering little serva came to look after me, and I reflected that after all this treatment showed confidence.

IV

Perhaps it did, but all the same, six weeks later, toward the middle of June, the moment when Mrs. Prest undertook her annual migration, I had made no measurable advance. I was obliged to confess to her that I had no results to speak of. My first step had been unexpectedly rapid, but there was no appearance that it would be followed by a second. I was a thousand miles from taking tea with my hostesses—that privilege of which, as I reminded Mrs. Prest, we both had had a vision. She reproached me with wanting boldness, and I answered that even to be bold you must have an opportunity: you may push on through a breach but you can't batter down a dead wall. She answered that the breach I had already made was big enough to admit an army and accused me of wasting precious hours in whimpering in her salon when I ought to have been carrying on the struggle in the field. It is true that I went to see her very often, on the theory that it would console me (I freely expressed my discouragement) for my want of success on my own premises. But I began to perceive that it did not console me to be perpetually chaffed for my scruples, especially when I was really so vigilant; and I was rather glad when my derisive friend closed her house for the summer. She had expected to gather amusement from the drama of my intercourse with the Misses Bordereau, and she was disappointed that the intercourse, and consequently the drama, had not come off. "They'll lead you on to your ruin," she said before she left Venice. "They'll get all your money without showing you a scrap." I think I settled down to my business with more concentration after she had gone away.

It was a fact that up to that time I had not, save on a single brief occasion, had even a moment's contact with my queer hostesses. The exception had occurred when I carried them according to my promise the terrible three thousand francs. Then I found Miss Tita waiting for me in the hall, and she took the money from my hand so that I did not see her aunt. The old lady had promised to receive me, but she apparently thought nothing of breaking that vow. The money was contained in a bag of chamois leather, of respectable dimensions, which my banker had given me, and Miss Tita had to make a big fist to receive it. This she did with extreme solemnity, though I tried to treat the affair a little as a joke. It was in no jocular strain, yet it was with simplicity, that she inquired, weighing the money in her two palms: "Don't you think it's too much?" To which I replied that that would depend upon the amount of pleasure I should get for it. Hereupon she turned away from me quickly, as she had done the day before, murmuring in a tone different from any she had used hitherto: "Oh, pleasure, pleasure—there's no pleasure in this house!"

After this, for a long time, I never saw her, and I wondered that the common chances of the day should not have helped us to meet. It could only be evident that she was immensely on her guard against them; and in addition to this the house was so big that for each other we were lost in it. I used to look out for her hopefully as I crossed the sala in my comings and goings, but I was not rewarded with a glimpse of the tail of her dress. It was as if she never peeped out of her aunt's apartment. I used to wonder what she did there week after week and year after year. I had never encountered such a violent parti pris of seclusion; it was more than keeping quiet—it was like hunted creatures feigning death. The two ladies appeared to have no visitors whatever and no sort of contact with the world. I judged at least that people could not have come to the house and that Miss Tita could not have gone out without my having some observation of it. I did what I disliked myself for doing (reflecting that it was only once in a way): I questioned my servant about their habits and let him divine that I should be interested in any information he could pick up. But he picked up amazingly little for a knowing Venetian: it must be added that where there is a perpetual fast there are very few crumbs on the floor. His cleverness in other ways was sufficient, if it was not quite all that I had attributed to him on the occasion of my first interview with Miss Tita. He had helped my gondolier to bring me round a boatload of furniture; and when these articles had been carried to the top of the palace and distributed according to our associated wisdom he organized my household with such promptitude as was consistent with the fact that it was composed exclusively of himself. He made me in short as comfortable as I could be with my indifferent prospects. I should have been glad if he had fallen in love with Miss Bordereau's maid or, failing this, had taken her in aversion; either event might have brought about some kind of catastrophe, and a catastrophe might have led to some parley. It was my idea that she would have been sociable, and I myself on various occasions saw her flit to and fro on domestic errands, so that I was sure she was accessible. But I tasted of no gossip from that fountain, and I afterward learned that Pasquale's affections were fixed upon an object that made him heedless of other women. This was a young lady with a powdered face, a yellow cotton gown, and much leisure, who used often to come to see him. She practiced, at her convenience, the art of a stringer of beads (these ornaments are made in Venice, in profusion; she had her pocket full of them, and I used to find them on the floor of my apartment), and kept an eye on the maiden in the house. It was not for me of course to make the domestics tattle, and I never said a word to Miss Bordereau's cook.

It seemed to me a proof of the old lady's determination to have nothing to do with me that she should never have sent me a receipt for my three months' rent. For some days I looked out for it and then, when I had given it up, I wasted a good deal of time in wondering what her reason had been for neglecting so indispensable and familiar a form. At first I was tempted to send her a reminder, after which I relinquished the idea (against my judgment as to what was right in the particular case), on the general ground of wishing to keep quiet. If Miss Bordereau suspected me of ulterior aims she would suspect me less if I should be businesslike, and yet I consented not to be so. It was possible she intended her omission as an impertinence, a visible irony, to show how she could overreach people who attempted to overreach her. On that hypothesis it was well to let her see that one did not notice her little tricks. The real reading of the matter, I afterward perceived, was simply the poor old woman's desire to emphasize the fact that I was in the enjoyment of a favor as rigidly limited as it had been liberally bestowed. She had given me part of her house, and now she would not give me even a morsel of paper with her name on it. Let me say that even at first this did not make me too miserable, for the whole episode was essentially delightful to me. I foresaw that I should have a summer after my own literary heart, and the sense of holding my opportunity was much greater than the sense of losing it. There could be no Venetian business without patience, and since I adored the place

I was much more in the spirit of it for having laid in a large provision. That spirit kept me perpetual company and seemed to look out at me from the revived immortal face—in which all his genius shone—of the great poet who was my prompter. I had invoked him and he had come; he hovered before me half the time; it was as if his bright ghost had returned to earth to tell me that he regarded the affair as his own no less than mine and that we should see it fraternally, cheerfully to a conclusion. It was as if he had said, "Poor dear, be easy with her; she has some natural prejudices; only give her time. Strange as it may appear to you she was very attractive in 1820. Meanwhile are we not in Venice together, and what better place is there for the meeting of dear friends? See how it glows with the advancing summer; how the sky and the sea and the rosy air and the marble of the palaces all shimmer and melt together." My eccentric private errand became a part of the general romance and the general glory—I felt even a mystic companionship, a moral fraternity with all those who in the past had been in the service of art. They had worked for beauty, for a devotion; and what else was I doing? That element was in everything that Jeffrey Aspern had written, and I was only bringing it to the light.

I lingered in the sala when I went to and fro; I used to watch—as long as I thought decent—the door that led to Miss Bordereau's part of the house. A person observing me might have supposed I was trying to cast a spell upon it or attempting some odd experiment in hypnotism. But I was only praying it would open or thinking what treasure probably lurked behind it. I hold it singular, as I look back, that I should never have doubted for a moment that the sacred relics were there; never have failed to feel a certain joy at being under the same roof with them. After all they were under my hand—they had not escaped me yet; and they made my life continuous, in a fashion, with the illustrious life they had touched at the other end. I lost myself in this satisfaction to the point of assuming—in my quiet extravagance—that poor Miss Tita also went back, went back, as I used to phrase it. She did indeed, the gentle spinster, but not quite so far as Jeffrey Aspern, who was simply hearsay to her, quite as he was to me. Only she had lived for years with Juliana, she had seen and handled the papers and (even though she was stupid) some esoteric knowledge had rubbed off on her. That was what the old woman represented—esoteric knowledge; and this was the idea with which my editorial heart used to thrill. It literally beat faster often, of an evening, when I had been out, as I stopped with my candle in the re-echoing hall on my way up to bed. It was as if at such a moment as that, in the stillness, after the long contradiction of the day, Miss Bordereau's secrets were in the air, the wonder of her survival more palpable. These were the acute impressions. I had them in another form, with more of a certain sort of reciprocity, during the hours that I sat in the garden looking up over the top of my book at the closed windows of my hostess. In these windows no sign of life ever appeared; it was as if, for fear of my catching a glimpse of them, the two ladies passed their days in the dark. But this only proved to me that they had something to conceal; which was what I had wished to demonstrate. Their motionless shutters became as expressive as eyes consciously closed, and I took comfort in thinking that at all events through invisible themselves they saw me between the lashes.

I made a point of spending as much time as possible in the garden, to justify the picture I had originally given of my horticultural passion. And I not only spent time, but (hang it! as I said) I spent money. As soon as I had got my rooms arranged and could give the proper thought to the matter I surveyed the place with a clever expert and made terms for having it put in order. I was sorry to do this, for personally I liked it better as it was, with its weeds and its wild, rough tangle, its sweet, characteristic Venetian shabbiness. I had to be consistent, to keep my promise that I would smother the house in flowers. Moreover I formed this graceful project that by flowers I would make my way—I would succeed by big nosegays. I would batter the old women with lilies—I would bombard their citadel with roses. Their door would have to yield to the pressure when a mountain of carnations should be piled up against it. The place in truth had been brutally neglected. The Venetian capacity for dawdling is of the largest, and for a good many days unlimited litter was all my gardener had to show for his ministrations. There was a great digging of holes and carting about of earth, and after a while I grew so impatient that I had thoughts of sending for my bouquets to the nearest stand. But I reflected that the ladies would see through the chinks of their shutters that they must have been bought and might make up their minds from this that I was a humbug. So I composed myself and finally, though the delay was long, perceived some appearances of bloom. This encouraged me, and I waited serenely enough till they multiplied. Meanwhile the real summer days arrived and began to pass, and as I look back upon them they seem to me almost the happiest of my life. I took more and more care to be in the garden whenever it was not too hot. I had an arbor arranged and a low table and an armchair put into it; and I carried out books and portfolios (I had always some business of writing in hand), and worked and waited and mused and hoped, while the golden hours elapsed and the plants drank in the light and the inscrutable old palace turned pale and then, as the day waned, began to flush in it and my papers rustled in the wandering breeze of the Adriatic.

Considering how little satisfaction I got from it at first it is remarkable that I should not have grown more tired of wondering what mystic rites of ennui the Misses Bordereau celebrated in their darkened rooms; whether this had always been the tenor of their life and how in previous years they had escaped elbowing their neighbors. It was clear that they must have had other habits and other circumstances; that they must once have been young or at least middle-aged. There was no end to the questions it was possible to ask about them and no end to the answers it was not possible to frame. I had known many of my country-people in Europe and was familiar with the strange ways they were liable to take up there; but the Misses Bordereau formed altogether a new type of the American absentee. Indeed it was plain that the American name had ceased to have any application to them—I had seen this in the ten minutes I spent in the old woman's room. You could never have said whence they came, from the appearance of either of them; wherever it was they had long ago dropped the local accent and fashion. There was nothing in them that one recognized, and putting the question of speech aside they might have been Norwegians or Spaniards. Miss Bordereau, after all, had been in Europe nearly three-quarters of a century; it appeared by some verses addressed to her by Aspern on the occasion of his own second absence from America—verses of which Cumnor and I had after infinite conjecture established solidly enough the date—that she was even then, as a girl of twenty, on the foreign side of the sea. There was an implication in the poem (I hope not just for the phrase) that he had come back for her sake. We had no real light upon her circumstances at that moment, any more than we had upon her origin, which we believed to be of the sort usually spoken of as modest. Cumnor had a theory that she had been a governess in some family in which the poet visited and that, in consequence of her position, there was from the first something unavowed, or rather something positively clandestine, in their relations. I on the other hand had hatched a little romance according to which she was the daughter of an artist, a painter or a sculptor, who had left the western world when the century was fresh, to study in the ancient schools. It was essential to my hypothesis that this amiable man should have lost his wife, should have been poor and unsuccessful and should have had a second daughter, of a disposition quite different from Juliana's. It was also indispensable that he should have been accompanied to Europe by these young ladies and should have established himself there for the remainder of a struggling, saddened life. There was a further implication that Miss Bordereau had had in her youth a perverse and adventurous, albeit a generous and fascinating character, and that she had passed through some singular vicissitudes. By what passions had she been ravaged, by what sufferings had she been blanched, what store of memories had she laid away for the monotonous future?

I asked myself these things as I sat spinning theories about her in my arbor and the bees droned in the flowers. It was incontestable that, whether for right or for wrong, most readers of certain of Aspern's poems (poems not as ambiguous as the sonnets—scarcely more divine, I think—of Shakespeare) had taken for granted that Juliana had not always adhered to the steep footway of renunciation. There hovered about her name a perfume of reckless passion, an intimation that she had not been exactly as the respectable young person in general. Was this a sign that her singer had betrayed her, had given her away, as we say nowadays, to posterity? Certain it is that it would have been difficult to put one's finger on the passage in which her fair fame suffered an imputation. Moreover was not any fame fair enough that was so sure of duration and was associated with works immortal through their beauty? It was a part of my idea that the young lady had had a foreign lover (and an unedifying tragical rupture) before her meeting with Jeffrey Aspern. She had lived with her father and sister in a queer old-fashioned, expatriated, artistic Bohemia, in the days when the aesthetic was only the academic and the painters who knew the best models for a contadina and pifferaro wore peaked hats and long hair. It was a society less furnished than the coteries of today (in its ignorance of the wonderful chances, the opportunities of the early bird, with which its path was strewn), with tatters of old stuff and fragments of old crockery; so that Miss Bordereau appeared not to have picked up or have inherited many objects of importance. There was no enviable bric-a-brac, with its provoking legend of cheapness, in the room in which I had seen her. Such a fact as that suggested bareness, but nonetheless it worked happily into the sentimental interest I had always taken in the early movements of my countrymen as visitors to Europe. When Americans went abroad in 1820 there was something romantic, almost heroic in it, as compared with the perpetual ferryings of the present hour, when photography and other conveniences have annihilated surprise. Miss Bordereau sailed with her family on a tossing brig, in the days of long voyages and sharp differences; she had her emotions on the top of yellow diligences, passed the night at inns where she dreamed of travelers' tales, and was struck, on reaching the Eternal City, with the elegance of Roman pearls and scarfs. There was something touching to me in all that, and my imagination frequently went back to the period. If Miss Bordereau carried it there of course Jeffrey Aspern at other times had done so a great deal more. It was a much more important fact, if one were looking at his genius critically, that he had lived in the days before the general transfusion. It had happened to me to regret that he had known Europe at all; I should have liked to see what he would have written without that experience, by which he had incontestably been enriched. But as his fate had ordered otherwise I went with him—I tried to judge how the Old World would have struck him. It was not only there, however, that I watched him; the relations he had entertained with the new had even a livelier interest. His own country after all had had most of his life, and his muse, as they said at that time, was essentially American. That was originally what I had loved him for: that at a period when our native land was nude and crude and provincial, when the famous "atmosphere" it is supposed to lack was not even missed, when literature was lonely there and art and form almost impossible, he had found means to live and write like one of the first; to be free and general and not at all afraid; to feel, understand, and express everything.

V

I was seldom at home in the evening, for when I attempted to occupy myself in my apartments the lamplight brought in a swarm of noxious insects, and it was too hot for closed windows. Accordingly I spent the late hours either on the water (the moonlight of Venice is famous), or in the splendid square which serves as a vast forecourt to the strange old basilica of Saint Mark. I sat in front of Florian's cafe, eating ices, listening to music, talking with acquaintances: the traveler will remember how the immense cluster of tables and little chairs stretches like a promontory into the smooth lake of the Piazza. The whole place, of a summer's evening, under the stars and with all the lamps, all the voices and light footsteps on marble (the only sounds of the arcades that enclose it), is like an open-air saloon dedicated to cooling drinks and to a still finer degustation—that of the exquisite impressions received during the day. When I did not prefer to keep mine to myself there was always a stray tourist, disencumbered of his Baedeker, to discuss them with, or some domesticated painter rejoicing in the return of the season of strong effects. The wonderful church, with its low domes and bristling embroideries, the mystery of its mosaic and sculpture, looking ghostly in the tempered gloom, and the sea breeze passed between the twin columns of the Piazzetta, the lintels of a door no longer guarded, as gently as if a rich curtain were swaying there. I used sometimes on these occasions to think of the Misses Bordereau and of the pity of their being shut up in apartments which in the Venetian July even Venetian vastness did not prevent from being stuffy. Their life seemed miles away from the life of the Piazza, and no doubt it was really too late to make the austere Juliana change her habits. But poor Miss Tita would have enjoyed one of Florian's ices, I was sure; sometimes I even had thoughts of carrying one home to her. Fortunately my patience bore fruit, and I was not obliged to do anything so ridiculous.

One evening about the middle of July I came in earlier than usual—I forget what chance had led to this—and instead of going up to my quarters made my way into the garden. The temperature was very high; it was such a night as one would gladly have spent in the open air, and I was in no hurry to go to bed. I had floated home in my gondola, listening to the slow splash of the oar in the narrow dark canals, and now the only thought that solicited me was the vague reflection that it would be pleasant to recline at one's length in the fragrant darkness on a garden bench. The odor of the canal was doubtless at the bottom of that aspiration and the breath of the garden, as I entered it, gave consistency to my purpose. It was delicious—just such an air as must have trembled with Romeo's vows when he stood among the flowers and raised his arms to his mistress's balcony. I looked at the windows of the palace to see if by chance the example of Verona (Verona being not far off) had been followed; but everything was dim, as usual, and everything was still. Juliana, on summer nights in her youth, might have murmured down from open windows at Jeffrey Aspern, but Miss Tita was not a poet's mistress any more than I was a poet. This however did not prevent my gratification from being great as I became aware on reaching the end of the garden that Miss Tita was seated in my little bower. At first I only made out an indistinct figure, not in the least counting on such an overture from one of my hostesses; it even occurred to me that some sentimental maidservant had stolen in to keep a tryst with her sweetheart. I was going to turn away, not to frighten her, when the figure rose to its height and I recognized Miss Bordereau's niece. I must do myself the justice to say that I did not wish to frighten her either, and much as I had longed for some such accident I should have been capable of retreating. It was as if I had laid a trap for her by coming home earlier than usual and adding to that eccentricity by creeping into the garden. As she rose she spoke to me, and then I reflected that perhaps, secure in my almost inveterate absence, it was her nightly practice to take a lonely airing. There was no trap, in truth, because I had had no suspicion. At first I took for granted that the words she uttered expressed discomfiture at my arrival; but as she repeated them—I had not caught them clearly—I had the surprise of hearing her say, "Oh, dear, I'm so very glad you've come!" She and her aunt had in common the property of unexpected speeches. She came out of the arbor almost as if she were going to throw herself into my arms.

I hasten to add that she did nothing of the kind; she did not even shake hands with me. It was a gratification to her to see me and presently she told me why—because she was nervous when she was out-of-doors at night alone. The plants and bushes looked so strange in the dark, and there were all sorts of queer sounds—she could not tell what they were—like the noises of animals. She stood close to me, looking about her with an air of greater security but without any demonstration of interest in me as an individual. Then I guessed that nocturnal prowlings were not in the least her habit, and I was also reminded (I had been struck with the circumstance in talking with her before I took possession) that it was impossible to overestimate her simplicity.

"You speak as if you were lost in the backwoods," I said, laughing. "How you manage to keep out of this charming place when you have only three steps to take to get into it is more than I have yet been able to discover. You hide away mighty well so long as I am on the premises, I know; but I had a hope that you peeped out a little at other times. You and your poor aunt are worse off than Carmelite nuns in their cells. Should you mind telling me how you exist without air, without exercise, without any sort of human contact? I don't see how you carry on the common business of life."

She looked at me as if I were talking some strange tongue, and her answer was so little of an answer that I was considerably irritated. "We go to bed very early—earlier than you would believe." I was on the point of saying that this only deepened the mystery when she gave me some relief by adding, "Before you came we were not so private. But I never have been out at night."

"Never in these fragrant alleys, blooming here under your nose?"

"Ah," said Miss Tita, "they were never nice till now!" There was an unmistakable reference in this and a flattering comparison, so that it seemed to me I had gained a small advantage. As it would help me to follow it up to establish a sort of grievance I asked her why, since she thought my garden nice, she had never thanked me in any way for the flowers I had been sending up in such quantities for the previous three weeks. I had not been discouraged—there had been, as she would have observed, a daily armful; but I had been brought up in the common forms and a word of recognition now and then would have touched me in the right place.

"Why I didn't know they were for me!"

“They were for both of you. Why should I make a difference?”

Miss Tita reflected as if she might by thinking of a reason for that, but she failed to produce one. Instead of this she asked abruptly, “Why in the world do you want to know us?”

“I ought after all to make a difference,” I replied. “That question is your aunt’s; it isn’t yours. You wouldn’t ask it if you hadn’t been put up to it.”

“She didn’t tell me to ask you,” Miss Tita replied without confusion; she was the oddest mixture of the shrinking and the direct.

“Well, she has often wondered about it herself and expressed her wonder to you. She has insisted on it, so that she has put the idea into your head that I am insufferably pushing. Upon my word I think I have been very discreet. And how completely your aunt must have lost every tradition of sociability, to see anything out of the way in the idea that respectable intelligent people, living as we do under the same roof, should occasionally exchange a remark! What could be more natural? We are of the same country, and we have at least some of the same tastes, since, like you, I am intensely fond of Venice.”

My interlocutress appeared incapable of grasping more than one clause in any proposition, and she declared quickly, eagerly, as if she were answering my whole speech: “I am not in the least fond of Venice. I should like to go far away!”

“Has she always kept you back so?” I went on, to show her that I could be as irrelevant as herself.

“She told me to come out tonight; she has told me very often,” said Miss Tita. “It is I who wouldn’t come. I don’t like to leave her.”

“Is she too weak, is she failing?” I demanded, with more emotion, I think, than I intended to show. I judged this by the way her eyes rested upon me in the darkness. It embarrassed me a little, and to turn the matter off I continued genially: “Do let us sit down together comfortably somewhere, and you will tell me all about her.”

Miss Tita made no resistance to this. We found a bench less secluded, less confidential, as it were, than the one in the arbor; and we were still sitting there when I heard midnight ring out from those clear bells of Venice which vibrate with a solemnity of their own over the lagoon and hold the air so much more than the chimes of other places. We were together more than an hour, and our interview gave, as it struck me, a great lift to my undertaking. Miss Tita accepted the situation without a protest; she had avoided me for three months, yet now she treated me almost as if these three months had made me an old friend. If I had chosen I might have inferred from this that though she had avoided me she had given a good deal of consideration to doing so. She paid no attention to the flight of time—never worried at my keeping her so long away from her aunt. She talked freely, answering questions and asking them and not even taking advantage of certain longish pauses with which they inevitably alternated to say she thought she had better go in. It was almost as if she were waiting for something—something I might say to her—and intended to give me my opportunity. I was the more struck by this as she told me that her aunt had been less well for a good many days and in a way that was rather new. She was weaker; at moments it seemed as if she had no strength at all; yet more than ever before she wished to be left alone. That was why she had told her to come out—not even to remain in her own room, which was alongside; she said her niece irritated her, made her nervous. She sat still for hours together, as if she were asleep; she had always done that, musing and dozing; but at such times formerly she gave at intervals some small sign of life, of interest, liking her companion to be near her with her work. Miss Tita confided to me that at present her aunt was so motionless that she sometimes feared she was dead; moreover she took hardly any food—one couldn't see what she lived on. The great thing was that she still on most days got up; the serious job was to dress her, to wheel her out of her bedroom. She clung to as many of her old habits as possible and she had always, little company as they had received for years, made a point of sitting in the parlor.

I scarcely knew what to think of all this—of Miss Tita's sudden conversion to sociability and of the strange circumstance that the more the old lady appeared to decline toward her end the less she should desire to be looked after. The story did not hang together, and I even asked myself whether it were not a trap laid for me, the result of a design to make me show my hand. I could not have told why my companions (as they could only by courtesy be called) should have this purpose—why they should try to trip up so lucrative a lodger. At any rate I kept on my guard, so that Miss Tita should not have occasion again to ask me if I had an arriere-pensee. Poor woman, before we parted for the night my mind was at rest as to HER capacity for entertaining one.

She told me more about their affairs than I had hoped; there was no need to be prying, for it evidently drew her out simply to feel that I listened, that I cared. She ceased wondering why I cared, and at last, as she spoke of the brilliant life they had led years before, she almost chattered. It was Miss Tita who judged it brilliant; she said that when they first came to live in Venice, years and years before (I saw that her mind was essentially vague about dates and the order in which events had occurred), there was scarcely a week that they had not some visitor or did not make some delightful passeggio in the city. They had seen all the curiosities; they had even been to the Lido in a boat (she spoke as if I might think there was a way on foot); they had had a collation there, brought in three baskets and spread out on the grass. I asked her what people they had known and she said, Oh! very nice ones—the Cavaliere Bombicci and the Contessa Altemura, with whom they had had a great friendship. Also English people—the Churtons and the Goldies and Mrs. Stock-Stock, whom they had loved dearly; she was dead and gone, poor dear. That was the case with most of their pleasant circle (this expression was Miss Tita's own), though a few were left, which was a wonder considering how they had neglected them. She mentioned the names of two or three Venetian old women; of a certain doctor, very clever, who was so kind—he came as a friend, he had really given up practice; of the avvocato Pochintesta, who wrote beautiful poems and had addressed one to her aunt. These people came to see them without fail every year, usually at the capo d'anno, and of old her aunt used to make them some little present—her aunt and she together: small things that she, Miss Tita, made herself, like paper lampshades or mats for the decanters of wine at dinner or those woolen things that in cold weather were worn on the wrists. The last few years there had not been many presents; she could not think what to make, and her aunt had lost her interest and never suggested. But the people came all the same; if the Venetians liked you once they liked you forever.

There was something affecting in the good faith of this sketch of former social glories; the picnic at the Lido had remained vivid through the ages, and poor Miss Tita evidently was of the impression that she had had a brilliant youth. She had in fact had a glimpse of the Venetian world in its gossiping, home-keeping, parsimonious, professional walks; for I observed for the first time that she had acquired by contact something of the trick of the familiar, soft-sounding, almost infantile speech of the place. I judged that she had imbibed this invertebrate dialect from the natural way the names of things and people—mostly purely local—rose to her lips. If she knew little of what they represented she knew still less of anything else. Her aunt had drawn in—her failing interest in the table mats and lampshades was a sign of that—and she had not been able to mingle in society or to entertain it alone; so that the matter of her reminiscences struck one as an old world altogether. If she had not been so decent her references would have seemed to carry one back to the queer rococo Venice of Casanova. I found myself falling into the error of thinking of her too as one of Jeffrey Aspern's contemporaries; this came from her having so little in common with my own. It was possible, I said to myself, that she had not even heard of him; it might very well be that Juliana had not cared to lift even for her the veil that covered the temple of her youth. In this case she perhaps would not know of the existence of the papers, and I welcomed that presumption—it made me feel more safe with her—until I remembered that we had believed the letter of disavowal received by Cumnor to be in the handwriting of the niece. If it had been dictated to her she had of course to know what it was about; yet after all the effect of it was to repudiate the idea of any connection with the poet. I held it probable at all events that Miss Tita had not read a word of his poetry. Moreover if, with her companion, she had always escaped the interviewer there was little occasion for her having got it into her head that people were "after" the letters. People had not been after them, inasmuch as they had not heard of them; and Cumnor's fruitless feeler would have been a solitary accident.

When midnight sounded Miss Tita got up; but she stopped at the door of the house only after she had wandered two or three times with me round the garden. "When shall I see you again?" I asked before she went in; to which she replied with promptness that she should like to come out the next night. She added however that she should not come—she was so far from doing everything she liked.

"You might do a few things that I like," I said with a sigh.

"Oh, you—I don't believe you!" she murmured at this, looking at me with her simple solemnity.

"Why don't you believe me?"

"Because I don't understand you."

"That is just the sort of occasion to have faith." I could not say more, though I should have liked to, as I saw that I only mystified her; for I had no wish to have it on my conscience that I might pass for having made love to her. Nothing less should I have seemed to do had I continued to beg a lady to "believe in me" in an Italian garden on a midsummer night. There was some merit in my scruples, for Miss Tita lingered and lingered: I perceived that she felt that she should not really soon come down again and wished therefore to protract the present. She insisted too on making the talk between us personal to ourselves; and altogether her behavior was such as would have been possible only to a completely innocent woman.

"I shall like the flowers better now that I know they are also meant for me."

"How could you have doubted it? If you will tell me the kind you like best I will send a double lot of them."

"Oh, I like them all best!" Then she went on, familiarly: "Shall you study—shall you read and write—when you go up to your rooms?"

"I don't do that at night, at this season. The lamplight brings in the animals."

"You might have known that when you came."

"I did know it!"

"And in winter do you work at night?"

"I read a good deal, but I don't often write." She listened as if these details had a rare interest, and suddenly a temptation quite at variance with the prudence I had been teaching myself associated itself with her plain, mild face. Ah yes, she was safe and I could make her safer! It seemed to me from one moment to another that I could not wait longer—that I really must take a sounding. So I went on: "In general before I go to sleep—very often in bed (it's a bad habit, but I confess to it), I read some great poet. In nine cases out of ten it's a volume of Jeffrey Aspern."

I watched her well as I pronounced that name but I saw nothing wonderful. Why should I indeed—was not Jeffrey Aspern the property of the human race?

"Oh, we read him—we HAVE read him," she quietly replied.

"He is my poet of poets—I know him almost by heart."

For an instant Miss Tita hesitated; then her sociability was too much for her.

"Oh, by heart—that's nothing!" she murmured, smiling. "My aunt used to know him—to know him"—she paused an instant and I wondered what she was going to say—"to know him as a visitor."

"As a visitor?" I repeated, staring.

"He used to call on her and take her out."

I continued to stare. "My dear lady, he died a hundred years ago!"

"Well," she said mirthfully, "my aunt is a hundred and fifty."

"Mercy on us!" I exclaimed; "why didn't you tell me before? I should like so to ask her about him."

"She wouldn't care for that—she wouldn't tell you," Miss Tita replied.

"I don't care what she cares for! She MUST tell me—it's not a chance to be lost."

"Oh, you should have come twenty years ago: then she still talked about him."

"And what did she say?" I asked eagerly.

"I don't know—that he liked her immensely."

"And she—didn't she like him?"

"She said he was a god." Miss Tita gave me this information flatly, without expression; her tone might have made it a piece of trivial gossip. But it stirred me deeply as she dropped the words into the summer night; it seemed such a direct testimony.

"Fancy, fancy!" I murmured. And then, "Tell me this, please—has she got a portrait of him? They are distressingly rare."

"A portrait? I don't know," said Miss Tita; and now there was discomfiture in her face. "Well, good night!" she added; and she turned into the house.

I accompanied her into the wide, dusky, stone-paved passage which on the ground floor corresponded with our grand sala. It opened at one end into the garden, at the other upon the canal, and was lighted now only by the small lamp that was always left for me to take up as I went to bed. An extinguished candle which Miss Tita apparently had brought down with her stood on the same table with it. "Good night, good night!" I replied, keeping beside her as she went to get her light. "Surely you would know, shouldn't you, if she had one?"

"If she had what?" the poor lady asked, looking at me queerly over the flame of her candle.

"A portrait of the god. I don't know what I wouldn't give to see it."

"I don't know what she has got. She keeps her things locked up." And Miss Tita went away, toward the staircase, with the sense evidently that she had said too much.

I let her go—I wished not to frighten her—and I contented myself with remarking that Miss Bordereau would not have locked up such a glorious possession as that—a thing a person would be proud of and hang up in a prominent place on the parlor wall. Therefore of course she had not any portrait. Miss Tita made no direct answer to this and, candle in hand, with her back to me, ascended two or three stairs. Then she stopped short and turned round, looking at me across the dusky space.

"Do you write—do you write?" There was a shake in her voice—she could scarcely bring out what she wanted to ask.

"Do I write? Oh, don't speak of my writing on the same day with Aspern's!"

"Do you write about HIM—do you pry into his life?"

"Ah, that's your aunt's question; it can't be yours!" I said, in a tone of slightly wounded sensibility.

"All the more reason then that you should answer it. Do you, please?"

I thought I had allowed for the falsehoods I should have to tell; but I found that in fact when it came to the point I had not. Besides, now that I had an opening there was a kind of relief in being frank. Lastly (it was perhaps fanciful, even fatuous), I guessed that Miss Tita personally would not in the last resort be less my friend. So after a moment's hesitation I answered, "Yes, I have written about him and I am looking for more material. In heaven's name have you got any?"

"Santo Dio!" she exclaimed, without heeding my question; and she hurried upstairs and out of sight. I might count upon her in the last resort, but for the present she was visibly alarmed. The proof of it was that she began to hide again, so that for a fortnight I never beheld her. I found my patience ebbing and after four or five days of this I told the gardener to stop the flowers.

VI

One afternoon, as I came down from my quarters to go out, I found Miss Tita in the sala: it was our first encounter on that ground since I had come to the house. She put on no air of being there by accident; there was an ignorance of such arts in her angular, diffident directness. That I might be quite sure she was waiting for me she informed me of the fact and told me that Miss Bordereau wished to see me: she would take me into the room at that moment if I had time. If I had been late for a love tryst I would have stayed for this, and I quickly signified that I should be delighted to wait upon the old lady. "She wants to talk with you—to know you," Miss Tita said, smiling as if she herself appreciated that idea; and she led me to the door of her aunt's apartment. I stopped her a moment before she had opened it, looking at her with some curiosity. I told her that this was a great satisfaction to me and a great honor; but all the same I should like to ask what had made Miss Bordereau change so suddenly. It was only the other day that she wouldn't suffer me near her. Miss Tita was not embarrassed by my question; she had as many little unexpected serenities as if she told fibs, but the odd part of them was that they had on the contrary their source in her truthfulness. "Oh, my aunt changes," she answered; "it's so terribly dull—I suppose she's tired."

"But you told me that she wanted more and more to be alone."

Poor Miss Tita colored, as if she found me over-insistent. "Well, if you don't believe she wants to see you—I haven't invented it! I think people often are capricious when they are very old."

"That's perfectly true. I only wanted to be clear as to whether you have repeated to her what I told you the other night."

"What you told me?"

"About Jeffrey Aspern—that I am looking for materials."

"If I had told her do you think she would have sent for you?"

"That's exactly what I want to know. If she wants to keep him to herself she might have sent for me to tell me so."

"She won't speak of him," said Miss Tita. Then as she opened the door she added in a lower tone, "I have told her nothing."

The old woman was sitting in the same place in which I had seen her last, in the same position, with the same mystifying bandage over her eyes. her welcome was to turn her almost invisible face to me and show me that while she sat silent she saw me clearly. I made no motion to shake hands with her; I felt too well on this occasion that that was out of place forever. It had been sufficiently enjoined upon me that she was too sacred for that sort of reciprocity—too venerable to touch. There was something so grim in her aspect (it was partly the accident of her green shade), as I stood there to be measured, that I ceased on the spot to feel any doubt as to her knowing my secret, though I did not in the least suspect that Miss Tita had not just spoken the truth. She had not betrayed me, but the old woman's brooding instinct had served her; she had turned me over and over in the long, still hours, and she had guessed. The worst of it was that she looked terribly like an old woman who at a pinch would burn her papers. Miss Tita pushed a chair forward, saying to me, "This will be a good place for you to sit." As I took possession of it I asked after Miss Bordereau's health; expressed the hope that in spite of the very hot weather it was satisfactory. She replied that it was good enough—good enough; that it was a great thing to be alive.

"Oh, as to that, it depends upon what you compare it with!" I exclaimed, laughing.

"I don't compare—I don't compare. If I did that I should have given everything up long ago."

I liked to think that this was a subtle allusion to the rapture she had known in the society of Jeffrey Aspern—though it was true that such an allusion would have accorded ill with the wish I imputed to her to keep him buried in her soul. What it accorded with was my constant conviction that no human being had ever had a more delightful social gift than his, and what it seemed to convey was that nothing in the world was worth speaking of if one pretended to speak of that. But one did not! Miss Tita sat down beside her aunt, looking as if she had reason to believe some very remarkable conversation would come off between us.

"It's about the beautiful flowers," said the old lady; "you sent us so many—I ought to have thanked you for them before. But I don't write letters and I receive only at long intervals."

She had not thanked me while the flowers continued to come, but she departed from her custom so far as to send for me as soon as she began to fear that they would not come any more. I noted this; I remembered what an acquisitive propensity she had shown when it was a question of extracting gold from me, and I privately rejoiced at the happy thought I had had in suspending my tribute. She had missed it and she was willing to make a concession to bring it back. At the first sign of this concession I could only go to meet her. "I am afraid you have not had many, of late, but they shall begin again immediately—tomorrow, tonight."

"Oh, do send us some tonight!" Miss Tita cried, as if it were an immense circumstance.

"What else should you do with them? It isn't a manly taste to make a bower of your room," the old woman remarked.

"I don't make a bower of my room, but I am exceedingly fond of growing flowers, of watching their ways. There is nothing unmanly in that: it has been the amusement of philosophers, of statesmen in retirement; even I think of great captains."

"I suppose you know you can sell them—those you don't use," Miss Bordereau went on. "I daresay they wouldn't give you much for them; still, you could make a bargain."

"Oh, I have never made a bargain, as you ought to know. My gardener disposes of them and I ask no questions."

"I would ask a few, I can promise you!" said Miss Bordereau; and it was the first time I had heard her laugh. I could not get used to the idea that this vision of pecuniary profit was what drew out the divine Juliana most.

"Come into the garden yourself and pick them; come as often as you like; come every day. They are all for you," I pursued, addressing Miss Tita and carrying off this veracious statement by treating it as an innocent joke. "I can't imagine why she doesn't come down," I added, for Miss Bordereau's benefit.

"You must make her come; you must come up and fetch her," said the old woman, to my stupefaction. "That odd thing you have made in the corner would be a capital place for her to sit."

The allusion to my arbor was irreverent; it confirmed the impression I had already received that there was a flicker of impertinence in Miss Bordereau's talk, a strange mocking lambency which must have been a part of her adventurous youth and which had outlived passions and faculties. Nonetheless I asked, "Wouldn't it be possible for you to come down there yourself? Wouldn't it do you good to sit there in the shade, in the sweet air?"

"Oh, sir, when I move out of this it won't be to sit in the air, and I'm afraid that any that may be stirring around me won't be particularly sweet! It will be a very dark shade indeed. But that won't be just yet," Miss Bordereau continued cannily, as if to correct any hopes that this courageous allusion to the last receptacle of her mortality might lead me to entertain. "I have sat here many a day and I have had enough of arbors in my time. But I'm not afraid to wait till I'm called."

Miss Tita had expected some interesting talk, but perhaps she found it less genial on her aunt's side (considering that I had been sent for with a civil intention) than she had hoped. As if to give the conversation a turn that would put our companion in a light more favorable she said to me, "Didn't I tell you the other night that she had sent me out? You see that I can do what I like!"

"Do you pity her—do you teach her to pity herself?" Miss Bordereau demanded before I had time to answer this appeal. "She has a much easier life than I had when I was her age."

"You must remember that it has been quite open to me to think you rather inhuman."

"Inhuman? That's what the poets used to call the women a hundred years ago. Don't try that; you won't do as well as they!" Juliana declared. "There is no more poetry in the world—that I know of at least. But I won't bandy words with you," she pursued, and I well remember the old-fashioned, artificial sound she gave to the speech. "You have made me talk, talk! It isn't good for me at all." I got up at this and told her I would take no more of her time; but she detained me to ask, "Do you remember, the day I saw you about the rooms, that you offered us the use of your gondola?" And when I assented, promptly, struck again with her disposition to make a "good thing" of being there and wondering what she now had in her eye, she broke out, "Why don't you take that girl out in it and show her the place?"

"Oh, dear Aunt, what do you want to do with me?" cried the "girl" with a piteous quaver. "I know all about the place!"

"Well then, go with him as a cicerone!" said Miss Bordereau with an effort of something like cruelty in her implacable power of retort—an incongruous suggestion that she was a sarcastic, profane, cynical old woman. "Haven't we heard that there have been all sorts of changes in all these years? You ought to see them and at your age (I don't mean because you're so young) you ought to take the chances that come. You're old enough, my dear, and this gentleman won't hurt you. He will show you the famous sunsets, if they still go on—DO they go on? The sun set for me so long ago. But that's not a reason. Besides, I shall never miss you; you think you are too important. Take her to the Piazza; it used to be very pretty," Miss Bordereau continued, addressing herself to me. "What have they done with the funny old church? I hope it hasn't tumbled down. Let her look at the shops; she may take some money, she may buy what she likes."

Poor Miss Tita had got up, discountenanced and helpless, and as we stood there before her aunt it would certainly have seemed to a spectator of the scene that the old woman was amusing herself at our expense. Miss Tita protested, in a confusion of exclamations and murmurs; but I lost no time in saying that if she would do me the honor to accept the hospitality of my boat I would engage that she should not be bored. Or if she did not want so much of my company the boat itself, with the gondolier, was at her service;

he was a capital oar and she might have every confidence. Miss Tita, without definitely answering this speech, looked away from me, out of the window, as if she were going to cry; and I remarked that once we had Miss Bordereau's approval we could easily come to an understanding. We would take an hour, whichever she liked, one of the very next days. As I made my obeisance to the old lady I asked her if she would kindly permit me to see her again.

For a moment she said nothing; then she inquired, "Is it very necessary to your happiness?"

"It diverts me more than I can say."

"You are wonderfully civil. Don't you know it almost kills ME?"

"How can I believe that when I see you more animated, more brilliant than when I came in?"

"That is very true, Aunt," said Miss Tita. "I think it does you good."

"Isn't it touching, the solicitude we each have that the other shall enjoy herself?" sneered Miss Bordereau. "If you think me brilliant today you don't know what you are talking about; you have never seen an agreeable woman. Don't try to pay me a compliment; I have been spoiled," she went on. "My door is shut, but you may sometimes knock."

With this she dismissed me, and I left the room. The latch closed behind me, but Miss Tita, contrary to my hope, had remained within. I passed slowly across the hall and before taking my way downstairs I waited a little. My hope was answered; after a minute Miss Tita followed me. "That's a delightful idea about the Piazza," I said. "When will you go—tonight, tomorrow?"

She had been disconcerted, as I have mentioned, but I had already perceived and I was to observe again that when Miss Tita was embarrassed she did not (as most women would have done) turn away from you and try to escape, but came closer, as it were, with a deprecating, clinging appeal to be spared, to be protected. Her attitude was perpetually a sort of prayer for assistance, for explanation; and yet no woman in the world could have been less of a comedian. From the moment you were kind to her she depended on you absolutely; her self-consciousness dropped from her and she took the greatest intimacy, the innocent intimacy which was the only thing she could conceive, for granted. She told me she did not know what had got into her aunt; she had changed so quickly, she had got some idea. I replied that she must find out what the idea was and then let me know; we would go and have an ice together at Florian's, and she should tell me while we listened to the band.

"Oh, it will take me a long time to find out!" she said, rather ruefully; and she could promise me this satisfaction neither for that night nor for the next. I was patient now, however, for I felt that I had only to wait; and in fact at the end of the week, one lovely evening after dinner, she stepped into my gondola, to which in honor of the occasion I had attached a second oar.

We swept in the course of five minutes into the Grand Canal; whereupon she uttered a murmur of ecstasy as fresh as if she had been a tourist just arrived. She had forgotten how splendid the great waterway looked on a clear, hot summer evening, and how the sense of floating between marble palaces and reflected lights disposed the mind to sympathetic talk. We floated long and far, and though Miss Tita gave no high-pitched voice to her satisfaction I felt that she surrendered herself. She was more than pleased, she was transported; the whole thing was an immense liberation. The gondola moved with slow strokes, to give her time to enjoy it, and she listened to the plash of the oars, which grew louder and more musically liquid as we passed into narrow canals, as if it were a revelation of Venice. When I asked her how long it was since she had been in a boat she answered, "Oh, I don't know; a long time—not since my aunt began to be ill." This was not the only example she gave me of her extreme vagueness about the previous years and the line which marked off the period when Miss Bordereau flourished. I was not at liberty to keep her out too long, but we took a considerable GIRO before going to the Piazza. I asked her no questions, keeping the conversation on purpose away from her domestic situation and the things I wanted to know; I poured treasures of information about Venice into her ears, described Florence and Rome, discoursed to her on the charms and advantages of travel. She reclined, receptive, on the deep leather cushions, turned her eyes conscientiously to everything I pointed out to her, and never mentioned to me till sometime afterward that she might be supposed to know Florence better than I, as she had lived there for years with Miss Bordereau. At last she asked, with the shy impatience of a child, "Are we not really going to the Piazza? That's what I want to see!" I immediately gave the order that we should go straight; and then we sat silent with the expectation of arrival. As some time still passed, however, she said suddenly, of her own movement, "I have found out what is the matter with my aunt: she is afraid you will go!"

"What has put that into her head?"

"She has had an idea you have not been happy. That is why she is different now."

"You mean she wants to make me happier?"

"Well, she wants you not to go; she wants you to stay."

"I suppose you mean on account of the rent," I remarked candidly.

Miss Tita's candor showed itself a match for my own. "Yes, you know; so that I shall have more."

"How much does she want you to have?" I asked, laughing. "She ought to fix the sum, so that I may stay till it's made up."

"Oh, that wouldn't please me," said Miss Tita. "It would be unheard of, your taking that trouble."

"But suppose I should have my own reasons for staying in Venice?"

"Then it would be better for you to stay in some other house."

"And what would your aunt say to that?"

"She wouldn't like it at all. But I should think you would do well to give up your reasons and go away altogether."

"Dear Miss Tita," I said, "it's not so easy to give them up!"

She made no immediate answer to this, but after a moment she broke out: "I think I know what your reasons are!"

"I daresay, because the other night I almost told you how I wish you would help me to make them good."

"I can't do that without being false to my aunt."

"What do you mean, being false to her?"

"Why, she would never consent to what you want. She has been asked, she has been written to. It made her fearfully angry."

"Then she HAS got papers of value?" I demanded quickly.

"Oh, she has got everything!" sighed Miss Tita with a curious weariness, a sudden lapse into gloom.

These words caused all my pulses to throb, for I regarded them as precious evidence. For some minutes I was too agitated to speak, and in the interval the gondola approached the Piazzetta. After we had disembarked I asked my companion whether she would rather walk round the square or go and sit at the door of the cafe; to which she replied that she would do whichever I liked best—I must only remember again how little time she had. I assured her there was plenty to do both, and we made the circuit of the long arcades. Her spirits revived at the sight of the bright shop windows, and she lingered and stopped, admiring or disapproving of their contents, asking me what I thought of things, theorizing about prices. My attention wandered from her; her words of a while before, "Oh, she has got everything!" echoed so in my consciousness. We sat down at last in the crowded circle at Florian's, finding an unoccupied table among those that were ranged in the square. It was a splendid night and all the world was out-of-doors; Miss Tita could not have wished the elements more auspicious for her return to society. I saw that she enjoyed it even more than she told; she was agitated with the multitude of her impressions. She had forgotten what an attractive thing the world is, and it was coming over her that somehow she had for the best years of her life been cheated of it. This did not make her angry; but as she looked all over the charming scene her face had, in spite of its smile of appreciation, the flush of a sort of wounded surprise. She became silent, as if she were thinking with a secret sadness of opportunities, forever lost, which ought to have been easy; and this gave me a chance to say to her, "Did you mean a while ago that your aunt has a plan of keeping me on by admitting me occasionally to her presence?"

"She thinks it will make a difference with you if you sometimes see her. She wants you so much to stay that she is willing to make that concession."

"And what good does she consider that I think it will do me to see her?"

"I don't know; she thinks it's interesting," said Miss Tita simply. "You told her you found it so."

"So I did; but everyone doesn't think so."

"No, of course not, or more people would try."

"Well, if she is capable of making that reflection she is capable of making this further one," I went on: "that I must have a particular reason for not doing as others do, in spite of the interest she offers—for not leaving her alone." Miss Tita looked as if she failed to grasp this rather complicated proposition; so I continued, "If you have not told her what I said to you the other night may she not at least have guessed it?"

"I don't know; she is very suspicious."

"But she has not been made so by indiscreet curiosity, by persecution?"

"No, no; it isn't that," said Miss Tita, turning on me a somewhat troubled face. "I don't know how to say it: it's on account of something—ages ago, before I was born—in her life."

"Something? What sort of thing?" I asked as if I myself could have no idea.

"Oh, she has never told me," Miss Tita answered; and I was sure she was speaking the truth.

Her extreme limpidity was almost provoking, and I felt for the moment that she would have been more satisfactory if she had been less ingenuous. "Do you suppose it's something to which Jeffrey Aspern's letters and papers—I mean the things in her possession—have reference?"

"I daresay it is!" my companion exclaimed as if this were a very happy suggestion. "I have never looked at any of those things."

"None of them? Then how do you know what they are?"

"I don't," said Miss Tita placidly. "I have never had them in my hands. But I have seen them when she has had them out."

"Does she have them out often?"

"Not now, but she used to. She is very fond of them."

"In spite of their being compromising?"

"Compromising?" Miss Tita repeated as if she was ignorant of the meaning of the word. I felt almost as one who corrupts the innocence of youth.

"I mean their containing painful memories."

"Oh, I don't think they are painful."

"You mean you don't think they affect her reputation?"

At this a singular look came into the face of Miss Bordereau's niece—a kind of confession of helplessness, an appeal to me to deal fairly, generously with her. I had brought her to the Piazza, placed her among charming influences, paid her an attention she appreciated, and now I seemed to let her perceive that all this had been a bribe—a bribe to make her turn in some way against her aunt. She was of a yielding nature and capable of doing almost anything to please a person who was kind to her; but the greatest kindness of all would be not to presume too much on this. It was strange enough, as I afterward thought, that she had not the least air of resenting my want of consideration for her aunt's character, which would have been in the worst possible taste if anything less vital (from my point of view) had been at stake.

I don't think she really measured it. "Do you mean that she did something bad?" she asked in a moment.

"Heaven forbid I should say so, and it's none of my business. Besides, if she did," I added, laughing, "it was in other ages, in another world. But why should she not destroy her papers?"

"Oh, she loves them too much."

"Even now, when she may be near her end?"

"Perhaps when she's sure of that she will."

"Well, Miss Tita," I said, "it's just what I should like you to prevent."

"How can I prevent it?"

"Couldn't you get them away from her?"

"And give them to you?"

This put the case very crudely, though I am sure there was no irony in her intention. "Oh, I mean that you might let me see them and look them over. It isn't for myself; there is no personal avidity in my desire. It is simply that they would be of such immense interest to the public, such immeasurable importance as a contribution to Jeffrey Aspern's history."

She listened to me in her usual manner, as if my speech were full of reference to things she had never heard of, and I felt particularly like the reporter of a newspaper who forces his way into a house of mourning. This was especially the case when after a moment she said. "There was a gentleman who some time ago wrote to her in very much those words. He also wanted her papers."

"And did she answer him?" I asked, rather ashamed of myself for not having her rectitude.

"Only when he had written two or three times. He made her very angry."

"And what did she say?"

"She said he was a devil," Miss Tita replied simply.

"She used that expression in her letter?"

"Oh, no; she said it to me. She made me write to him."

"And what did you say?"

"I told him there were no papers at all."

"Ah, poor gentleman!" I exclaimed.

"I knew there were, but I wrote what she bade me."

"Of course you had to do that. But I hope I shall not pass for a devil."

"It will depend upon what you ask me to do for you," said Miss Tita, smiling.

"Oh, if there is a chance of YOUR thinking so my affair is in a bad way! I shan't ask you to steal for me, nor even to fib—for you can't fib, unless on paper. But the principal thing is this—to prevent her from destroying the papers."

"Why, I have no control of her," said Miss Tita. "It's she who controls me."

"But she doesn't control her own arms and legs, does she? The way she would naturally destroy her letters would be to burn them. Now she can't burn them without fire, and she can't get fire unless you give it to her."

"I have always done everything she has asked," my companion rejoined. "Besides, there's Olimpia."

I was on the point of saying that Olimpia was probably corruptible, but I thought it best not to sound that note. So I simply inquired if that faithful domestic could not be managed.

"Everyone can be managed by my aunt," said Miss Tita. And then she observed that her holiday was over; she must go home.

I laid my hand on her arm, across the table, to stay her a moment. "What I want of you is a general promise to help me."

"Oh, how can I—how can I?" she asked, wondering and troubled. She was half-surprised, half-frightened at my wishing to make her play an active part.

"This is the main thing: to watch her carefully and warn me in time, before she commits that horrible sacrilege."

"I can't watch her when she makes me go out."

"That's very true."

"And when you do, too."

"Mercy on us; do you think she will have done anything tonight?"

"I don't know; she is very cunning."

"Are you trying to frighten me?" I asked.

I felt this inquiry sufficiently answered when my companion murmured in a musing, almost envious way, "Oh, but she loves them—she loves them!"

This reflection, repeated with such emphasis, gave me great comfort; but to obtain more of that balm I said, "If she shouldn't intend to destroy the objects we speak of before her death she will probably have made some disposition by will."

"By will?"

"Hasn't she made a will for your benefit?"

"Why, she has so little to leave. That's why she likes money," said Miss Tita.

"Might I ask, since we are really talking things over, what you and she live on?"

"On some money that comes from America, from a lawyer. He sends it every quarter. It isn't much!"

"And won't she have disposed of that?"

My companion hesitated—I saw she was blushing. "I believe it's mine," she said; and the look and tone which accompanied these words betrayed so the absence of the habit of thinking of herself that I almost thought her charming. The next instant she added, "But she had a lawyer once, ever so long ago. And some people came and signed something."

"They were probably witnesses. And you were not asked to sign? Well then," I argued rapidly and hopefully, "it is because you are the legatee; she has left all her documents to you!"

"If she has it's with very strict conditions," Miss Tita responded, rising quickly, while the movement gave the words a little character of decision. They seemed to imply that the bequest would be accompanied with a command that the articles bequeathed should remain concealed from every inquisitive eye and that I was very much mistaken if I thought she was the person to depart from an injunction so solemn.

"Oh, of course you will have to abide by the terms," I said; and she uttered nothing to mitigate the severity of this conclusion. Nonetheless, later, just before we disembarked at her own door, on our return, which had taken place almost in silence, she said to me abruptly, "I will do what I can to help you." I was grateful for this—it was very well so far as it went; but it did not keep me from remembering that night in a worried waking hour that I now had her word for it to reinforce my own impression that the old woman was very cunning.

VII

The fear of what this side of her character might have led her to do made me nervous for days afterward. I waited for an intimation from Miss Tita; I almost figured to myself that it was her duty to keep me informed, to let me know definitely whether or no Miss Bordereau had sacrificed her treasures. But as she gave no sign I lost patience and determined to judge so far as was possible with my own senses. I sent late one afternoon to ask if I might pay the ladies a visit, and my servant came back with surprising news. Miss Bordereau could be approached without the least difficulty; she had been moved out into the sala and was sitting by the window that overlooked the garden. I descended and found this picture correct; the old lady had been wheeled forth into the world and had a certain air, which came mainly perhaps from some brighter element in her dress, of being prepared again to have converse with it. It had not yet, however, begun to flock about her; she was perfectly alone and, though the door leading to her own quarters stood open, I had at first no glimpse of Miss Tita. The window at which she sat had the afternoon shade and, one of the shutters having been pushed back, she could see the pleasant garden, where the summer sun had by this time dried up too many of the plants—she could see the yellow light and the long shadows.

"Have you come to tell me that you will take the rooms for six months more?" she asked as I approached her, startling me by something coarse in her cupidity almost as much as if she had not already given me a specimen of it. Juliana's desire to make our acquaintance lucrative had been, as I have sufficiently indicated, a false note in my image of the woman who had inspired a great poet with immortal lines; but I may say here definitely that I recognized after all that it behooved me to make a large allowance for her. It was I who had kindled the unholy flame; it was I who had put into her head that she had the means of making money. She appeared never to have thought of that; she had been living wastefully for years, in a house five times too big for her, on a footing that I could explain only by the presumption that, excessive as it was, the space she enjoyed cost her next to nothing and that small as were her revenues they left her, for Venice, an appreciable margin. I had descended on her one day and taught her to calculate, and my almost extravagant comedy on the subject of the garden had presented me irresistibly in the light of a victim. Like all persons who achieve the miracle of changing their point of view when they are old she had been intensely converted; she had seized my hint with a desperate, tremulous clutch.

I invited myself to go and get one of the chairs that stood, at a distance, against the wall (she had given herself no concern as to whether I should sit or stand); and while I placed it near her I began, gaily, "Oh, dear madam, what an imagination you have, what an intellectual sweep! I am a poor devil of a man of letters who lives from day to day. How can I take palaces by the year? My existence is precarious. I don't know whether six months hence I shall have bread to put in my mouth. I have treated myself for once; it has been an immense luxury. But when it comes to going on—!"

"Are your rooms too dear? If they are you can have more for the same money," Juliana responded. "We can arrange, we can combinare, as they say here."

"Well yes, since you ask me, they are too dear," I said. "Evidently you suppose me richer than I am."

She looked at me in her barricaded way. "If you write books don't you sell them?"

"Do you mean don't people buy them? A little—not so much as I could wish. Writing books, unless one be a great genius—and even then!—is the last road to fortune. I think there is no more money to be made by literature."

"Perhaps you don't choose good subjects. What do you write about?" Miss Bordereau inquired.

"About the books of other people. I'm a critic, an historian, in a small way." I wondered what she was coming to.

"And what other people, now?"

"Oh, better ones than myself: the great writers mainly—the great philosophers and poets of the past; those who are dead and gone and can't speak for themselves."

"And what do you say about them?"

"I say they sometimes attached themselves to very clever women!" I answered, laughing. I spoke with great deliberation, but as my words fell upon the air they struck me as imprudent. However, I risked them and I was not sorry, for perhaps after all the old woman would be willing to treat. It seemed to be tolerably obvious that she knew my secret: why therefore drag the matter out? But she did not take what I had said as a confession; she only asked:

"Do you think it's right to rake up the past?"

"I don't know that I know what you mean by raking it up; but how can we get at it unless we dig a little? The present has such a rough way of treading it down."

"Oh, I like the past, but I don't like critics," the old woman declared with her fine tranquility.

"Neither do I, but I like their discoveries."

"Aren't they mostly lies?"

"The lies are what they sometimes discover," I said, smiling at the quiet impertinence of this. "They often lay bare the truth."

"The truth is God's, it isn't man's; we had better leave it alone. Who can judge of it—who can say?"

"We are terribly in the dark, I know," I admitted; "but if we give up trying what becomes of all the fine things? What becomes of the work I just mentioned, that of the great philosophers and poets? It is all vain words if there is nothing to measure it by."

"You talk as if you were a tailor," said Miss Bordereau whimsically; and then she added quickly, in a different manner, "This house is very fine; the proportions are magnificent. Today I wanted to look at this place again. I made them bring me out here. When your man came, just now, to learn if I would see you, I was on the point of sending for you, to ask if you didn't mean to go on. I wanted to judge what I'm letting you have. This sala is very grand," she pursued, like an auctioneer, moving a little, as I guessed, her invisible eyes. "I don't believe you often have lived in such a house, eh?"

"I can't often afford to!" I said.

"Well then, how much will you give for six months?"

I was on the point of exclaiming—and the air of excruciation in my face would have denoted a moral face—"Don't, Juliana; for HIS sake, don't!" But I controlled myself and asked less passionately: "Why should I remain so long as that?"

"I thought you liked it," said Miss Bordereau with her shriveled dignity.

"So I thought I should."

For a moment she said nothing more, and I left my own words to suggest to her what they might. I half-expected her to say, coldly enough, that if I had been disappointed we need not continue the discussion, and this in spite of the fact that I believed her now to have in her mind (however it had come there) what would have told her that my disappointment was natural. But to my extreme surprise she ended by observing: "If you don't think we have treated you well enough perhaps we can discover some way of treating you better." This speech was somehow so incongruous that it made me laugh again, and I excused myself by saying that she talked as if I were a sulky boy, pouting in the corner, to be "brought round." I had not a grain of complaint to make; and could anything have exceeded Miss Tita's graciousness in accompanying me a few nights before to the Piazza? At this the old woman went on: "Well, you brought it on yourself!" And then in a different tone, "She is a very nice girl." I assented cordially to this proposition, and she expressed the hope that I did so not merely to be obliging, but that I really liked her. Meanwhile I wondered still more what Miss Bordereau was coming to. "Except for me, today," she said, "she has not a relation in the world." Did she by describing her niece as amiable and unencumbered wish to represent her as a parti?

It was perfectly true that I could not afford to go on with my rooms at a fancy price and that I had already devoted to my undertaking almost all the hard cash I had set apart for it. My patience and my time were by no means exhausted, but I should be able to draw upon them only on a more usual Venetian basis. I was willing to pay the venerable woman with whom my pecuniary dealings were such a discord twice as much as any other padrona di casa would have asked, but I was not willing to pay her twenty times as much. I told her so plainly, and my plainness appeared to have some success, for she exclaimed, "Very good; you have done what I asked—you have made an offer!"

"Yes, but not for half a year. Only by the month."

"Oh, I must think of that then." She seemed disappointed that I would not tie myself to a period, and I guessed that she wished both to secure me and to discourage me; to say severely, "Do you dream that you can get off with less than six months? Do you dream that even by the end of that time you will be appreciably nearer your victory?" What was more in my mind was that she had a fancy to play me the trick of making me engage myself when in fact she had annihilated the papers. There was a moment when my suspense on this point was so acute that I all but broke out with the question, and what kept it back was but a kind of instinctive recoil (lest it should be a mistake), from the last violence of self-exposure. She was such a subtle old witch that one could never tell where one stood with her. You may imagine whether it cleared up the puzzle when, just after she had said she would think of my proposal and without any formal transition, she drew out of her pocket with an embarrassed hand a small object wrapped in crumpled white paper. She held it there a moment and then she asked, "Do you know much about curiosities?"

"About curiosities?"

"About antiquities, the old gimcracks that people pay so much for today. Do you know the kind of price they bring?"

I thought I saw what was coming, but I said ingenuously, "Do you want to buy something?"

"No, I want to sell. What would an amateur give me for that?" She unfolded the white paper and made a motion for me to take from her a small oval portrait. I possessed myself of it with a hand of which I could only hope that she did not perceive the tremor, and she added, "I would part with it only for a good price."

At the first glance I recognized Jeffrey Aspern, and I was well aware that I flushed with the act. As she was watching me however I had the consistency to exclaim, "What a striking face! Do tell me who it is."

"It's an old friend of mine, a very distinguished man in his day. He gave it to me himself, but I'm afraid to mention his name, lest you never should have heard of him, critic and historian as you are. I know the world goes fast and one generation forgets another. He was all the fashion when I was young."

She was perhaps amazed at my assurance, but I was surprised at hers; at her having the energy, in her state of health and at her time of life, to wish to sport with me that way simply for her private entertainment—the humor to test me and practice on me. This, at least, was the interpretation that I put upon her production of the portrait, for I could not believe that she really desired to sell it or cared for any information I might give her. What she wished was to dangle it before my eyes and put a prohibitive price on it. "The face comes back to me, it torments me," I said, turning the object this way and that and looking at it very critically. It was a careful but not a supreme work of art, larger than the ordinary miniature and representing a young man with a remarkably handsome face, in a high-collared green coat and a buff waistcoat. I judged the picture to have a valuable quality of resemblance and to have been painted when the model was about twenty-five years old. There are, as all the world knows, three other portraits of the poet in existence, but none of them is of so early a date as this elegant production. "I have never seen the original but I have seen other likenesses," I went on. "You expressed doubt of this generation having heard of the gentleman, but he strikes me for all the world as a celebrity. Now who is he? I can't put my finger on him—I can't give him a label. Wasn't he a writer? Surely he's a poet." I was determined that it should be she, not I, who should first pronounce Jeffrey Aspern's name.

My resolution was taken in ignorance of Miss Bordereau's extremely resolute character, and her lips never formed in my hearing the syllables that meant so much for her. She neglected to answer my question but raised her hand to take back the picture, with a gesture which though ineffectual was in a high degree peremptory. "It's only a person who should know for himself that would give me my price," she said with a certain dryness.

"Oh, then, you have a price?" I did not restore the precious thing; not from any vindictive purpose but because I instinctively clung to it. We looked at each other hard while I retained it.

"I know the least I would take. What it occurred to me to ask you about is the most I shall be able to get."

She made a movement, drawing herself together as if, in a spasm of dread at having lost her treasure, she were going to attempt the immense effort of rising to snatch it from me. I instantly placed it in her hand again, saying as I did so, "I should like to have it myself, but with your ideas I could never afford it."

She turned the small oval plate over in her lap, with its face down, and I thought I saw her catch her breath a little, as if she had had a strain or an escape. This however did not prevent her saying in a moment, "You would buy a likeness of a person you don't know, by an artist who has no reputation?"

"The artist may have no reputation, but that thing is wonderfully well painted," I replied, to give myself a reason.

"It's lucky you thought of saying that, because the painter was my father."

"That makes the picture indeed precious!" I exclaimed, laughing; and I may add that a part of my laughter came from my satisfaction in finding that I had been right in my theory of Miss Bordereau's origin. Aspern had of course met the young lady when he went to her father's studio as a sitter. I observed to Miss Bordereau that if she would entrust me with her property for twenty-four hours I should be happy to take advice upon it; but she made no answer to this save to slip it in silence into her pocket. This convinced me still more that she had no sincere intention of selling it during her lifetime, though she may have desired to satisfy herself as to the sum her niece, should she leave it to her, might expect eventually to obtain for it. "Well, at any rate I hope you will not offer it without giving me notice," I said as she remained irresponsive. "Remember that I am a possible purchaser."

"I should want your money first!" she returned with unexpected rudeness; and then, as if she bethought herself that I had just cause to complain of such an insinuation and wished to turn the matter off, asked abruptly what I talked about with her niece when I went out with her that way in the evening.

"You speak as if we had set up the habit," I replied. "Certainly I should be very glad if it were to become a habit. But in that case I should feel a still greater scruple at betraying a lady's confidence."

"Her confidence? Has she got confidence?"

"Here she is—she can tell you herself," I said; for Miss Tita now appeared on the threshold of the old woman's parlor. "Have you got confidence, Miss Tita? Your aunt wants very much to know."

"Not in her, not in her!" the younger lady declared, shaking her head with a dolefulness that was neither jocular not affected. "I don't know what to do with her; she has fits of horrid imprudence. She is so easily tired—and yet she has begun to roam—to drag herself about the house." And she stood looking down at her immemorial companion with a sort of helpless wonder, as if all their years of familiarity had not made her perversities, on occasion, any more easy to follow.

"I know what I'm about. I'm not losing my mind. I daresay you would like to think so," said Miss Bordereau with a cynical little sigh.

"I don't suppose you came out here yourself. Miss Tita must have had to lend you a hand," I interposed with a pacifying intention.

"Oh, she insisted that we should push her; and when she insists!" said Miss Tita in the same tone of apprehension; as if there were no knowing what service that she disapproved of her aunt might force her next to render.

"I have always got most things done I wanted, thank God! The people I have lived with have humored me," the old woman continued, speaking out of the gray ashes of her vanity.

"I suppose you mean that they have obeyed you."

"Well, whatever it is, when they like you."

"It's just because I like you that I want to resist," said Miss Tita with a nervous laugh.

"Oh, I suspect you'll bring Miss Bordereau upstairs next to pay me a visit," I went on; to which the old lady replied:

"Oh, no; I can keep an eye on you from here!"

"You are very tired; you will certainly be ill tonight!" cried Miss Tita.

"Nonsense, my dear; I feel better at this moment than I have done for a month. Tomorrow I shall come out again. I want to be where I can see this clever gentleman."

"Shouldn't you perhaps see me better in your sitting room?" I inquired.

"Don't you mean shouldn't you have a better chance at me?" she returned, fixing me a moment with her green shade.

"Ah, I haven't that anywhere! I look at you but I don't see you."

"You excite her dreadfully—and that is not good," said Miss Tita, giving me a reproachful, appealing look.

"I want to watch you—I want to watch you!" the old lady went on.

"Well then, let us spend as much of our time together as possible—I don't care where—and that will give you every facility."

"Oh, I've seen you enough for today. I'm satisfied. Now I'll go home." Miss Tita laid her hands on the back of her aunt's chair and began to push, but I begged her to let me take her place. "Oh, yes, you may move me this way—you shan't in any other!" Miss Bordereau exclaimed as she felt herself propelled firmly and easily over the smooth, hard floor. Before we reached the door of her own apartment she commanded me to stop, and she took a long, last look up and down the noble sala. "Oh, it's a magnificent house!" she murmured; after which I pushed her forward. When we had entered the parlor Miss Tita told me that she should now be able to manage, and at the same moment the little red-haired donna came to meet her mistress. Miss Tita's idea was evidently to get her aunt immediately back to bed. I confess that in spite of this urgency I was guilty of the indiscretion of lingering; it held me there to think that I was nearer the documents I coveted—that they were probably put away somewhere in the faded, unsociable room. The place had indeed a bareness which did not suggest hidden treasures; there were no dusky nooks nor curtained corners, no massive cabinets nor chests with iron bands. Moreover it was possible, it was perhaps even probable that the old lady had consigned her relics to her bedroom, to some battered box that was shoved under the bed, to the drawer of some lame dressing table, where they would be in the range of vision by the dim night lamp. Nonetheless I scrutinized every article of furniture, every conceivable cover for a hoard, and noticed that there were half a dozen things with drawers, and in particular a tall old secretary, with brass ornaments of the style of the Empire—a receptacle somewhat rickety but still capable of keeping a great many secrets. I don't know why this article fascinated me so, inasmuch as I certainly had no definite purpose of breaking into it; but I stared at it so hard that Miss Tita noticed me and changed color. Her doing this made me think I was right and that wherever they might have been before the Aspern papers at that moment languished behind the peevish little lock of the secretary. It was hard to remove my eyes from the dull mahogany front when I reflected that a simple panel divided me from the goal of my hopes; but I remembered my prudence and with an effort took leave of Miss Bordereau. To make the effort graceful I said to her that I should certainly bring her an opinion about the little picture.

"The little picture?" Miss Tita asked, surprised.

"What do YOU know about it, my dear?" the old woman demanded. "You needn't mind. I have fixed my price."

"And what may that be?"

"A thousand pounds."

"Oh Lord!" cried poor Miss Tita irrepressibly.

"Is that what she talks to you about?" said Miss Bordereau.

"Imagine your aunt's wanting to know!" I had to separate from Miss Tita with only those words, though I should have liked immensely to add, "For heaven's sake meet me tonight in the garden!"

VIII

As it turned out the precaution had not been needed, for three hours later, just as I had finished my dinner, Miss Bordereau's niece appeared, unannounced, in the open doorway of the room in which my simple repasts were served. I remember well that I felt no surprise at seeing her; which is not a proof that I did not believe in her timidity. It was immense, but in a case in which there was a particular reason for boldness it never would have prevented her from running up to my rooms. I saw that she was now quite full of a particular reason; it threw her forward—made her seize me, as I rose to meet her, by the arm.

"My aunt is very ill; I think she is dying!"

"Never in the world," I answered bitterly. "Don't you be afraid!"

"Do go for a doctor—do, do! Olimpia is gone for the one we always have, but she doesn't come back; I don't know what has happened to her. I told her that if he was not at home she was to follow him where he had gone; but apparently she is following him all over Venice. I don't know what to do—she looks so as if she were sinking."

"May I see her, may I judge?" I asked. "Of course I shall be delighted to bring someone; but hadn't we better send my man instead, so that I may stay with you?"

Miss Tita assented to this and I dispatched my servant for the best doctor in the neighborhood. I hurried downstairs with her, and on the way she told me that an hour after I quitted them in the afternoon Miss Bordereau had had an attack of "oppression," a terrible difficulty in breathing. This had subsided but had left her so exhausted that she did not come up: she seemed all gone. I repeated that she was not gone, that she would not go yet; whereupon Miss Tita gave me a sharper sidelong glance than she had ever directed at me and said, "Really, what do you mean? I suppose you don't accuse her of making believe!" I forget what reply I made to this, but I grant that in my heart I thought the old woman capable of any weird maneuver. Miss Tita wanted to know what I had done to her; her aunt had told her that I had made her so angry. I declared I had done nothing—I had been exceedingly careful; to which my companion rejoined that Miss Bordereau had assured her she had had a scene with me—a scene that had upset her. I answered with some resentment that it was a scene of her own making—that I couldn't think what she was angry with me for unless for not seeing my way to give a thousand pounds for the portrait of Jeffrey Aspern. "And did she show you that? Oh, gracious—oh, deary me!" groaned Miss Tita, who appeared to feel that the situation was passing out of her control and that the elements of her fate were thickening around her. I said that I would give anything to possess it, yet that I had not a thousand pounds; but I stopped when we came to the door of Miss Bordereau's room. I had an immense curiosity to pass it, but I thought it my duty to represent to Miss Tita that if I made the invalid angry she ought perhaps to be spared the sight of me. "The sight of you? Do you think she can SEE?" my companion demanded almost with indignation. I did think so but forebore to say it, and I softly followed my conductress.

I remember that what I said to her as I stood for a moment beside the old woman's bed was, "Does she never show you her eyes then? Have you never seen them?" Miss Bordereau had been divested of her green shade, but (it was not my fortune to behold Juliana in her nightcap) the upper half of her face was covered by the fall of a piece of dingy lacelike muslin, a sort of extemporized hood which, wound round her head, descended to the end of her nose, leaving nothing visible but her white withered cheeks and puckered mouth, closed tightly and, as it were consciously. Miss Tita gave me a glance of surprise, evidently not seeing a reason for my impatience. "You mean that she always wears something? She does it to preserve them."

"Because they are so fine?"

"Oh, today, today!" And Miss Tita shook her head, speaking very low. "But they used to be magnificent!"

"Yes indeed, we have Aspern's word for that." And as I looked again at the old woman's wrappings I could imagine that she had not wished to allow people a reason to say that the great poet had overdone it. But I did not waste my time in considering Miss Bordereau, in whom the appearance of respiration was so slight as to suggest that no human attention could ever help her more. I turned my eyes all over the room, rummaging with them the closets, the chests of drawers, the tables. Miss Tita met them quickly and read, I think, what was in them; but she did not answer it, turning away restlessly, anxiously, so that I felt rebuked, with reason, for a preoccupation that was almost profane in the presence of our dying companion. All the same I took another look, endeavoring to pick out mentally the place to try first, for a person who should wish to put his hand on Miss Bordereau's papers directly after her death. The room was a dire confusion; it looked like the room of an old actress. There were clothes hanging over chairs, odd-looking shabby bundles here and there, and various pasteboard boxes piled together, battered, bulging, and discolored, which might have been fifty years old. Miss Tita after a moment noticed the direction of my eyes again and, as if she guessed how I judged the air of the place (forgetting I had no business to judge it at all), said, perhaps to defend herself from the imputation of complicity in such untidiness:

"She likes it this way; we can't move things. There are old bandboxes she has had most of her life." Then she added, half taking pity on my real thought, "Those things were THERE." And she pointed to a small, low trunk which stood under a sofa where there was just room for it. It appeared to be a queer, superannuated coffer, of painted wood, with elaborate handles and shriveled straps and with the color (it had last been endued with a coat of light green) much rubbed off. It evidently had traveled with Juliana in the olden time—in the days of her adventures, which it had shared. It would have made a strange figure arriving at a modern hotel.

"WERE there—they aren't now?" I asked, startled by Miss Tita's implication.

She was going to answer, but at that moment the doctor came in—the doctor whom the little maid had been sent to fetch and whom she had at last overtaken. My servant, going on his own errand, had met her with her companion in tow, and in the sociable Venetian spirit, retracing his steps with them, had also come up to the threshold of Miss Bordereau's room, where I saw him peeping over the doctor's shoulder. I motioned him away the more instantly that the sight of his prying face reminded me that I myself had almost as little to do there—an admonition confirmed by the sharp way the little doctor looked at me, appearing to take me for a rival who had the field before him. He was a short, fat, brisk gentleman who wore the tall hat of his profession and seemed to look at everything but his patient. He looked particularly at me, as if it struck him that I should be better for a dose, so that I bowed to him and left him with the women, going down to smoke a cigar in the garden. I was nervous; I could not go further; I could not leave the place. I don't know exactly what I thought might happen, but it seemed to me important to be there. I wandered about in the alleys—the warm night had come on—smoking cigar after cigar and looking at the light in Miss Bordereau's windows. They were open now, I could see; the situation was different. Sometimes the light moved, but not quickly; it did not suggest the hurry of a crisis. Was the old woman dying, or was she already dead? Had the doctor said that there was nothing to be done at her tremendous age but to let her quietly pass away; or had he simply announced with a look a little more conventional that the end of the end had come? Were the other two women moving about to perform the offices that follow in such a case? It made me uneasy not to be nearer, as if I thought the doctor himself might carry away the papers with him. I bit my cigar hard as it came over me again that perhaps there were now no papers to carry!

I wandered about for an hour—for an hour and a half. I looked out for Miss Tita at one of the windows, having a vague idea that she might come there to give me some sign. Would she not see the red tip of my cigar moving about in the dark and feel that I wanted eminently to know what the doctor had said? I am afraid it is a proof my anxieties had made me gross that I should have taken in some degree for granted that at such an hour, in the midst of the greatest change that could take place in her life, they were uppermost also in Miss Tita's mind. My servant came down and spoke to me; he knew nothing save that the doctor had gone after a visit of half an hour. If he had stayed half an hour then Miss Bordereau was still alive: it could not have taken so much time as that to enunciate the contrary. I sent the man out of the house; there were moments when the sense of his curiosity annoyed me, and this was one of them. HE had been watching my cigar tip from an upper window, if Miss Tita had not; he could not know what I was after and I could not tell him, though I was conscious he had fantastic private theories about me which he thought fine and which I, had I known them, should have thought offensive.

I went upstairs at last but I ascended no higher than the sala. The door of Miss Bordereau's apartment was open, showing from the parlor the dimness of a poor candle. I went toward it with a light tread, and at the same moment Miss Tita appeared and stood looking at me as I approached. "She's better—she's better," she said, even before I had asked. "The doctor has given her something; she woke up, came back to life while he was there. He says there is no immediate danger."

"No immediate danger? Surely he thinks her condition strange!"

"Yes, because she had been excited. That affects her dreadfully."

"It will do so again then, because she excites herself. She did so this afternoon."

"Yes; she mustn't come out any more," said Miss Tita, with one of her lapses into a deeper placidity.

"What is the use of making such a remark as that if you begin to rattle her about again the first time she bids you?"

"I won't—I won't do it any more."

"You must learn to resist her," I went on.

"Oh, yes, I shall; I shall do so better if you tell me it's right."

"You mustn't do it for me; you must do it for yourself. It all comes back to you, if you are frightened."

"Well, I am not frightened now," said Miss Tita cheerfully. "She is very quiet."

"Is she conscious again—does she speak?"

"No, she doesn't speak, but she takes my hand. She holds it fast."

"Yes," I rejoined, "I can see what force she still has by the way she grabbed that picture this afternoon. But if she holds you fast how comes it that you are here?"

Miss Tita hesitated a moment; though her face was in deep shadow (she had her back to the light in the parlor and I had put down my own candle far off, near the door of the sala), I thought I saw her smile ingenuously. "I came on purpose—I heard your step."

"Why, I came on tiptoe, as inaudibly as possible."

"Well, I heard you," said Miss Tita.

"And is your aunt alone now?"

"Oh, no; Olimpia is sitting there."

On my side I hesitated. "Shall we then step in there?" And I nodded at the parlor; I wanted more and more to be on the spot.

"We can't talk there—she will hear us."

I was on the point of replying that in that case we would sit silent, but I was too conscious that this would not do, as there was something I desired immensely to ask her. So I proposed that we should walk a little in the sala, keeping more at the other end, where we should not disturb the old lady. Miss Tita assented unconditionally; the doctor was coming again, she said, and she would be there to meet him at the door. We strolled through the fine superfluous hall, where on the marble floor—particularly as at first we said nothing—our footsteps were more audible than I had expected. When we reached the other end—the wide window, inveterately closed, connecting with the balcony that overhung the canal—I suggested that we should remain there, as she would see the doctor arrive still better. I opened the window and we passed out on the balcony. The air of the canal seemed even heavier, hotter than that of the sala. The place was hushed and void; the quiet neighborhood had gone to sleep. A lamp, here and there, over the narrow black water, glimmered in double; the voice of a man going homeward singing, with his jacket on his shoulder and his hat on his ear, came to us from a distance. This did not prevent the scene from being very comme il faut, as Miss Bordereau had called it the first time I saw her. Presently a gondola passed along the canal with its slow rhythmical plash, and as we listened we watched it in silence. It did not stop, it did not carry the doctor; and after it had gone on I said to Miss Tita:

"And where are they now—the things that were in the trunk?"

"In the trunk?"

"That green box you pointed out to me in her room. You said her papers had been there; you seemed to imply that she had transferred them."

"Oh, yes; they are not in the trunk," said Miss Tita.

"May I ask if you have looked?"

"Yes, I have looked—for you."

"How for me, dear Miss Tita? Do you mean you would have given them to me if you had found them?" I asked, almost trembling.

She delayed to reply and I waited. Suddenly she broke out, "I don't know what I would do—what I wouldn't!"

"Would you look again—somewhere else?"

She had spoken with a strange unexpected emotion, and she went on in the same tone: "I can't—I can't—while she lies there. It isn't decent."

"No, it isn't decent," I replied gravely. "Let the poor lady rest in peace." And the words, on my lips, were not hypocritical, for I felt reprimanded and shamed.

Miss Tita added in a moment, as if she had guessed this and were sorry for me, but at the same time wished to explain that I did drive her on or at least did insist too much: "I can't deceive her that way. I can't deceive her—perhaps on her deathbed."

"Heaven forbid I should ask you, though I have been guilty myself!"

"You have been guilty?"

"I have sailed under false colors." I felt now as if I must tell her that I had given her an invented name, on account of my fear that her aunt would have heard of me and would refuse to take me in. I explained this and also that I had really been a party to the letter written to them by John Cumnor months before.

She listened with great attention, looking at me with parted lips, and when I had made my confession she said, "Then your real name—what is it?" She repeated it over twice when I had told her, accompanying it with the exclamation "Gracious, gracious!" Then she added, "I like your own best."

"So do I," I said, laughing. "Ouf! it's a relief to get rid of the other."

"So it was a regular plot—a kind of conspiracy?"

"Oh, a conspiracy—we were only two," I replied, leaving out Mrs. Prest of course.

She hesitated; I thought she was perhaps going to say that we had been very base. But she remarked after a moment, in a candid, wondering way, "How much you must want them!"

"Oh, I do, passionately!" I conceded, smiling. And this chance made me go on, forgetting my compunction of a moment before. "How can she possibly have changed their place herself? How can she walk? How can she arrive at that sort of muscular exertion? How can she lift and carry things?"

"Oh, when one wants and when one has so much will!" said Miss Tita, as if she had thought over my question already herself and had simply had no choice but that answer—the idea that in the dead of night, or at some moment when the coast was clear, the old woman had been capable of a miraculous effort.

"Have you questioned Olimpia? Hasn't she helped her—hasn't she done it for her?" I asked; to which Miss Tita replied promptly and positively that their servant had had nothing to do with the matter, though without admitting definitely that she had spoken to her. It was as if she were a little shy, a little ashamed now of letting me see how much she had entered into my uneasiness and had me on her mind. Suddenly she said to me, without any immediate relevance:

"I feel as if you were a new person, now that you have got a new name."

"It isn't a new one; it is a very good old one, thank heaven!"

She looked at me a moment. "I do like it better."

"Oh, if you didn't I would almost go on with the other!"

"Would you really?"

I laughed again, but for all answer to this inquiry I said, "Of course if she can rummage about that way she can perfectly have burnt them."

"You must wait—you must wait," Miss Tita moralized mournfully; and her tone ministered little to my patience, for it seemed after all to accept that wretched possibility. I would teach myself to wait, I declared nevertheless; because in the first place I could not do otherwise and in the second I had her promise, given me the other night, that she would help me.

"Of course if the papers are gone that's no use," she said; not as if she wished to recede, but only to be conscientious.

"Naturally. But if you could only find out!" I groaned, quivering again.

"I thought you said you would wait."

"Oh, you mean wait even for that?"

"For what then?"

"Oh, nothing," I replied, rather foolishly, being ashamed to tell her what had been implied in my submission to delay—the idea that she would do more than merely find out. I know not whether she guessed this; at all events she appeared to become aware of the necessity for being a little more rigid.

"I didn't promise to deceive, did I? I don't think I did."

"It doesn't much matter whether you did or not, for you couldn't!"

I don't think Miss Tita would have contested this event had she not been diverted by our seeing the doctor's gondola shoot into the little canal and approach the house. I noted that he came as fast as if he believed that Miss Bordereau was still in danger. We looked down at him while he disembarked and then went back into the sala to meet him. When he came up however I naturally left Miss Tita to go off with him alone, only asking her leave to come back later for news.

I went out of the house and took a long walk, as far as the Piazza, where my restlessness declined to quit me. I was unable to sit down (it was very late now but there were people still at the little tables in front of the cafes); I could only walk round and round, and I did so half a dozen times. I was uncomfortable, but it gave me a certain pleasure to have told Miss Tita who I really was. At last I took my way home again, slowly getting all but inextricably lost, as I did whenever I went out in Venice: so that it was considerably past midnight when I reached my door. The sala, upstairs, was as dark as usual and my lamp as I crossed it found nothing satisfactory to show me. I was disappointed, for I had notified Miss Tita that I would come back for a report, and I thought she might have left a light there as a sign. The door of the ladies' apartment was closed; which seemed an intimation that my faltering friend had gone to bed, tired of waiting for me. I stood in the middle of the place, considering, hoping she would hear me and perhaps peep out, saying to myself too that she would never go to bed with her aunt in a state so critical; she would sit up and watch—she would be in a chair, in her dressing gown. I went nearer the door; I stopped there and listened. I heard nothing at all and at last I tapped gently. No answer came and after another minute I turned the handle. There was no light in the room; this ought to have prevented me from going in, but it had no such effect. If I have candidly narrated the importunities, the indelicacies, of which my desire to possess myself of Jeffrey Aspern's papers had rendered me capable I need not shrink from confessing this last indiscretion. I think it was the worst thing I did; yet there were extenuating circumstances. I was deeply though doubtless not disinterestedly anxious for more news of the old lady, and Miss Tita had accepted from me, as it were, a rendezvous which it might have been a point of honor with me to keep. It may be said that her leaving the place dark was a positive sign that she released me, and to this I can only reply that I desired not to be released.

The door of Miss Bordereau's room was open and I could see beyond it the faintness of a taper. There was no sound—my footstep caused no one to stir. I came further into the room; I lingered there with my lamp in my hand. I wanted to give Miss Tita a chance to come to me if she were with her aunt, as she must be. I made no noise to call her; I only waited to see if she would not notice my light. She did not, and I explained this (I found afterward I was right) by the idea that she had fallen asleep. If she had fallen asleep her aunt was not on her mind, and my explanation ought to have led me to go out as I had come. I must repeat again that it did not, for I found myself at the same moment thinking of something else. I had no definite purpose, no bad intention, but I felt myself held to the spot by an acute, though absurd, sense of opportunity. For what I could not have said, inasmuch as it was not in my mind that I might commit a theft. Even if it had been I was confronted with the evident fact that Miss Bordereau did not leave her secretary, her cupboard, and the drawers of her tables gaping. I had no keys, no tools, and no ambition to smash her furniture. Nonetheless it came to me that I was now, perhaps alone, unmolested, at the hour of temptation and secrecy, nearer to the tormenting treasure than I had ever been. I held up my lamp, let the light play on the different objects as if it could tell me something. Still there came no movement from the other room. If Miss Tita was sleeping she was sleeping sound. Was she doing so—generous creature—on purpose to leave me the field? Did she know I was there and was she just keeping quiet to see what I would do—what I COULD do? But what could I do, when it came to that? She herself knew even better than I how little.

I stopped in front of the secretary, looking at it very idiotically; for what had it to say to me after all? In the first place it was locked, and in the second it almost surely contained nothing in which I was interested. Ten to one the papers had been destroyed; and even if they had not been destroyed the old woman would not have put them in such a place as that after removing them from the green trunk—would not have transferred them, if she had the idea of their safety on her brain, from the better hiding place to the worse. The secretary was more conspicuous, more accessible in a room in which she could no longer mount guard. It opened with a key, but there was a little brass handle, like a button, as well; I saw this as I played my lamp over it. I did something more than this at that moment: I caught a glimpse of the possibility that Miss Tita wished me really to understand. If she did not wish me to understand, if she wished me to keep away, why had she not locked the door of communication between the sitting room and the sala? That would have been a definite sign that I was to leave them alone. If I did not leave them alone she meant me to come for a purpose—a purpose now indicated by the quick, fantastic idea that to oblige me she had unlocked the secretary. She had not left the key, but the lid would probably move if I touched the button. This theory fascinated me, and I bent over very close to judge. I did not propose to do anything, not even—not in the least—to let down the lid; I only wanted to test my theory, to see if the cover WOULD move. I touched the button with my hand—a mere touch would tell me; and as I did so (it is embarrassing for me to relate it), I looked over my shoulder. It was a chance, an instinct, for I had not heard anything. I almost let my luminary drop and certainly I stepped back, straightening myself up at what I saw. Miss Bordereau stood there in her nightdress, in the doorway of her room, watching me; her hands were raised, she had lifted the everlasting curtain that covered half her face, and for the first, the last, the only time I beheld her extraordinary eyes. They glared at me, they made me horribly ashamed. I never shall forget her strange little bent white tottering figure, with its lifted head, her attitude, her expression; neither shall I forget the tone in which as I turned, looking at her, she hissed out passionately, furiously:

"Ah, you publishing scoundrel!"

I know not what I stammered, to excuse myself, to explain; but I went toward her, to tell her I meant no harm. She waved me off with her old hands, retreating before me in horror; and the next thing I knew she had fallen back with a quick spasm, as if death had descended on her, into Miss Tita's arms.

IX

I left Venice the next morning, as soon as I learned that the old lady had not succumbed, as I feared at the moment, to the shock I had given her—the shock I may also say she had given me. How in the world could I have supposed her capable of getting out of bed by herself? I failed to see Miss Tita before going; I only saw the donna, whom I entrusted with a note for her younger mistress. In this note I mentioned that I should be absent but for a few days. I went to Treviso, to Bassano, to Castelfranco; I took walks and drives and looked at musty old churches with ill-lighted pictures and spent hours seated smoking at the doors of cafes, where there were flies and yellow curtains, on the shady side of sleepy little squares. In spite of these pastimes, which were mechanical and perfunctory, I scantily enjoyed my journey: there was too strong a taste of the disagreeable in my life. I had been devilish awkward, as the young men say, to be found by Miss Bordereau in the dead of night examining the attachment of her bureau; and it had not been less so to have to believe for a good many hours afterward that it was highly probable I had killed her. In writing to Miss Tita I attempted to minimize these irregularities; but as she gave me no word of answer I could not know what impression I made upon her. It rankled in my mind that I had been called a publishing scoundrel, for certainly I did publish and certainly I had not been very delicate. There was a moment when I stood convinced that the only way to make up for this latter fault was to take myself away altogether on the instant; to sacrifice my hopes and relieve the two poor women forever of the oppression of my intercourse. Then I reflected that I had better try a short absence first, for I must already have had a sense (unexpressed and dim) that in disappearing completely it would not be merely my own hopes that I should condemn to extinction. It would perhaps be sufficient if I stayed away long enough to give the elder lady time to think she was rid of me. That she would wish to be rid of me after this (if I was not rid of her) was now not to be doubted: that nocturnal scene would have cured her of the disposition to put up with my company for the sake of my dollars. I said to myself that after all I could not abandon Miss Tita, and I continued to say this even while I observed that she quite failed to comply with my earnest request (I had given her two or three addresses, at little towns, post restante) that she would let me know how she was getting on. I would have made my servant write to me but that he was unable to manage a pen. It struck me there was a kind of scorn in Miss Tita's silence (little disdainful as she had ever been), so that I was uncomfortable and sore. I had scruples about going back and yet I had others about not doing so, for I wanted to put myself on a better footing. The end of it was that I did return to Venice on the twelfth day; and as my gondola gently bumped against Miss Bordereau's steps a certain palpitation of suspense told me that I had done myself a violence in holding off so long.

I had faced about so abruptly that I had not telegraphed to my servant. He was therefore not at the station to meet me, but he poked out his head from an upper window when I reached the house. "They have put her into the earth, la vecchia," he said to me in the lower hall, while he shouldered my valise; and he grinned and almost winked, as if he knew I should be pleased at the news.

"She's dead!" I exclaimed, giving him a very different look.

"So it appears, since they have buried her."

"It's all over? When was the funeral?"

"The other yesterday. But a funeral you could scarcely call it, signore; it was a dull little passeggio of two gondolas. Poveretta!" the man continued, referring apparently to Miss Tita. His conception of funerals was apparently that they were mainly to amuse the living.

I wanted to know about Miss Tita—how she was and where she was—but I asked him no more questions till we had got upstairs. Now that the fact had met me I took a bad view of it, especially of the idea that poor Miss Tita had had to manage by herself after the end. What did she know about arrangements, about the steps to take in such a case? Poveretta indeed! I could only hope that the doctor had given her assistance and that she had not been neglected by the old friends of whom she had told me, the little band of the faithful whose fidelity consisted in coming to the house once a year. I elicited from my servant that two old ladies and an old gentleman had in fact rallied round Miss Tita and had supported her (they had come for her in a gondola of their own) during the journey to the cemetery, the little red-walled island of tombs which lies to the north of the town, on the way to Murano. It appeared from these circumstances that the Misses Bordereau were Catholics, a discovery I had never made, as the old woman could not go to church and her niece, so far as I perceived, either did not or went only to early mass in the parish, before I was stirring. Certainly even the priests respected their seclusion; I had never caught the whisk of the curato's skirt. That evening, an hour later, I sent my servant down with five words written on a card, to ask Miss Tita if she would see me for a few moments. She was not in the house, where he had sought her, he told me when he came back, but in the garden walking about to refresh herself and gathering flowers. He had found her there and she would be very happy to see me.

I went down and passed half an hour with poor Miss Tita. She had always had a look of musty mourning (as if she were wearing out old robes of sorrow that would not come to an end), and in this respect there was no appreciable change in her appearance. But she evidently had been crying, crying a great deal—simply, satisfyingly, refreshingly, with a sort of primitive, retarded sense of loneliness and violence. But she had none of the formalism or the self-consciousness of grief, and I was almost surprised to see her standing there in the first dusk with her hands full of flowers, smiling at me with her reddened eyes. Her white face, in the frame of her mantilla, looked longer, leaner than usual. I had had an idea that she would be a good deal disgusted with me—would consider that I ought to have been on the spot to advise her, to help her; and, though I was sure there was no rancor in her composition and no great conviction of the importance of her affairs, I had prepared myself for a difference in her manner, for some little injured look, half-familiar, half-estranged, which should say to my conscience, "Well, you are a nice person to have professed things!" But historic truth compels me to declare that Tita Bordereau's countenance expressed unqualified pleasure in seeing her late aunt's lodger. That touched him extremely, and he thought it simplified his situation until he found it did not. I was as kind to her that evening as I knew how to be, and I walked about the garden with her for half an hour. There was no explanation of any sort between us; I did not ask her why she had not answered my letter. Still less did I repeat what I had said to her in that communication; if she chose to let me suppose that she had forgotten the position in which Miss Bordereau surprised me that night and the effect of the discovery on the old woman I was quite willing to take it that way: I was grateful to her for not treating me as if I had killed her aunt.

We strolled and strolled and really not much passed between us save the recognition of her bereavement, conveyed in my manner and in a visible air that she had of depending on me now, since I let her see that I took an interest in her. Miss Tita had none of the pride that makes a person wish to preserve the look of independence; she did not in the least pretend that she knew at present what would become of her. I forebore to touch particularly on that, however, for I certainly was not prepared to say that I would take charge of her. I was cautious; not ignobly, I think, for I felt that her knowledge of life was so small that in her unsophisticated vision there would be no reason why—since I seemed to pity her—I should not look after her. She told me how her aunt had died, very peacefully at the last, and how everything had been done afterward by the care of her good friends (fortunately, thanks to me, she said, smiling, there was money in the house; and she repeated that when once the Italians like you they are your friends for life); and when we had gone into this she asked me about my giro, my impressions, the places I had seen. I told her what I could, making it up partly, I am afraid, as in my depression I had not seen much; and after she had heard me she exclaimed, quite as if she had forgotten her aunt and her sorrow, "Dear, dear, how much I should like to do such things—to take a little journey!" It came over me for the moment that I ought to propose some tour, say I would take her anywhere she liked; and I remarked at any rate that some excursion—to give her a change—might be managed: we would think of it, talk it over. I said never a word to her about the Aspern documents; asked no questions as to what she had ascertained or what had otherwise happened with regard to them before Miss Bordereau's death. It was not that I was not on pins and needles to know, but that I thought it more decent not to betray my anxiety so soon after the catastrophe. I hoped she herself would say something, but she never glanced that way, and I thought this natural at the time. Later however, that night, it occurred to me that her silence was somewhat strange; for if she had talked of my movements, of anything so detached as the Giorgione at Castelfranco, she might have alluded to what she could easily remember was in my mind. It was not to be supposed that the emotion produced by her aunt's death had blotted out the recollection that I was interested in that lady's relics, and I fidgeted afterward as it came to me that her reticence might very possibly mean simply that nothing had been found. We separated in the garden (it was she who said she must go in); now that she was alone in the rooms I felt that (judged, at any rate, by Venetian ideas) I was on rather a different footing in regard to visiting her there. As I shook hands with her for goodnight I asked her if she had any general plan—had thought over what she had better do. "Oh, yes, oh, yes, but I haven't settled anything yet," she replied quite cheerfully. Was her cheerfulness explained by the impression that I would settle for her?

I was glad the next morning that we had neglected practical questions, for this gave me a pretext for seeing her again immediately. There was a very practical question to be touched upon. I owed it to her to let her know formally that of course I did not expect her to keep me on as a lodger, and also to show some interest in her own tenure, what she might have on her hands in the way of a lease. But I was not destined, as it happened, to converse with her for more than an instant on either of these points. I sent her no message; I simply went down to the sala and walked to and fro there. I knew she would come out; she would very soon discover I was there. Somehow I preferred not to be shut up with her; gardens and big halls seemed better places to talk. It was a splendid morning, with something in the air that told of the waning of the long Venetian summer; a freshness from the sea which stirred the flowers in the garden and made a pleasant draught in the house, less shuttered and darkened now than when the old woman was alive. It was the beginning of autumn, of the end of the golden months. With this it was the end of my experiment—or would be in the course of half an hour, when I should really have learned that the papers had been reduced to ashes. After that there would be nothing left for me but to go to the station; for seriously (and as it struck me in the morning light) I could not linger there to act as guardian to a piece of middle-aged female helplessness. If she had not saved the papers wherein should I be indebted to her? I think I winced a little as I asked myself how much, if she HAD saved them, I should have to recognize and, as it were, to reward such a courtesy. Might not that circumstance after all saddle me with a guardianship? If this idea did not make me more uncomfortable as I walked up and down it was because I was convinced I had nothing to look to. If the old woman had not destroyed everything before she pounced upon me in the parlor she had done so afterward.

It took Miss Tita rather longer than I had expected to guess that I was there; but when at last she came out she looked at me without surprise. I said to her that I had been waiting for her, and she asked why I had not let her know. I was glad the next day that I had checked myself before remarking that I had wished to see if a friendly intuition would not tell her: it became a satisfaction to me that I had not indulged in that rather tender joke. What I did say was virtually the truth—that I was too nervous, since I expected her now to settle my fate.

"Your fate?" said Miss Tita, giving me a queer look; and as she spoke I noticed a rare change in her. She was different from what she had been the evening before—less natural, less quiet. She had been crying the day before and she was not crying now, and yet she struck me as less confident. It was as if something had happened to her during the night, or at least as if she had thought of something that troubled her—something in particular that affected her relations with me, made them more embarrassing and complicated. Had she simply perceived that her aunt's not being there now altered my position?

"I mean about our papers. ARE there any? You must know now."

"Yes, there are a great many; more than I supposed." I was struck with the way her voice trembled as she told me this.

"Do you mean that you have got them in there—and that I may see them?"

"I don't think you can see them," said Miss Tita with an extraordinary expression of entreaty in her eyes, as if the dearest hope she had in the world now was that I would not take them from her. But how could she expect me to make such a sacrifice as that after all that had passed between us? What had I come back to Venice for but to see them, to take them? My delight in learning they were still in existence was such that if the poor woman had gone down on her knees to beseech me never to mention them again I would have treated the proceeding as a bad joke. "I have got them but I can't show them," she added.

"Not even to me? Ah, Miss Tita!" I groaned, with a voice of infinite remonstrance and reproach.

She colored, and the tears came back to her eyes; I saw that it cost her a kind of anguish to take such a stand but that a dreadful sense of duty had descended upon her. It made me quite sick to find myself confronted with that particular obstacle; all the more that it appeared to me I had been extremely encouraged to leave it out of account. I almost considered that Miss Tita had assured me that if she had no greater hindrance than that—! "You don't mean to say you made her a deathbed promise? It was precisely against your doing anything of that sort that I thought I was safe. Oh, I would rather she had burned the papers outright than that!"

"No, it isn't a promise," said Miss Tita.

"Pray what is it then?"

She hesitated and then she said, "She tried to burn them, but I prevented it. She had hid them in her bed."

"In her bed?"

"Between the mattresses. That's where she put them when she took them out of the trunk. I can't understand how she did it, because Olimpia didn't help her. She tells me so, and I believe her. My aunt only told her afterward, so that she shouldn't touch the bed—anything but the sheets. So it was badly made," added Miss Tita simply.

"I should think so! And how did she try to burn them?"

"She didn't try much; she was too weak, those last days. But she told me—she charged me. Oh, it was terrible! She couldn't speak after that night; she could only make signs."

"And what did you do?"

"I took them away. I locked them up."

"In the secretary?"

"Yes, in the secretary," said Miss Tita, reddening again.

"Did you tell her you would burn them?"

"No, I didn't—on purpose."

"On purpose to gratify me?"

"Yes, only for that."

"And what good will you have done me if after all you won't show them?"

"Oh, none; I know that—I know that."

"And did she believe you had destroyed them?"

"I don't know what she believed at the last. I couldn't tell—she was too far gone."

"Then if there was no promise and no assurance I can't see what ties you."

"Oh, she hated it so—she hated it so! She was so jealous. But here's the portrait—you may have that," Miss Tita announced, taking the little picture, wrapped up in the same manner in which her aunt had wrapped it, out of her pocket.

"I may have it—do you mean you give it to me?" I questioned, staring, as it passed into my hand.

"Oh, yes."

"But it's worth money—a large sum."

"Well!" said Miss Tita, still with her strange look.

I did not know what to make of it, for it could scarcely mean that she wanted to bargain like her aunt. She spoke as if she wished to make me a present. "I can't take it from you as a gift," I said, "and yet I can't afford to pay you for it according to the ideas Miss Bordereau had of its value. She rated it at a thousand pounds."

"Couldn't we sell it?" asked Miss Tita.

"God forbid! I prefer the picture to the money."

"Well then keep it."

"You are very generous."

"So are you."

"I don't know why you should think so," I replied; and this was a truthful speech, for the singular creature appeared to have some very fine reference in her mind, which I did not in the least seize.

"Well, you have made a great difference for me," said Miss Tita.

I looked at Jeffrey Aspern's face in the little picture, partly in order not to look at that of my interlocutress, which had begun to trouble me, even to frighten me a little—it was so self-conscious, so unnatural. I made no answer to this last declaration; I only privately consulted Jeffrey Aspern's delightful eyes with my own (they were so young and brilliant, and yet so wise, so full of vision); I asked him what on earth was the matter with Miss Tita. He seemed to smile at me with friendly mockery, as if he were amused at my case. I had got into a pickle for him—as if he needed it! He was unsatisfactory, for the only moment since I had known him. Nevertheless, now that I held the little picture in my hand I felt that it would be a precious possession. "Is this a bribe to make me give up the papers?" I demanded in a moment, perversely. "Much as I value it, if I were to be obliged to choose, the papers are what I should prefer. Ah, but ever so much!"

"How can you choose—how can you choose?" Miss Tita asked, slowly, lamentably.

"I see! Of course there is nothing to be said, if you regard the interdiction that rests upon you as quite insurmountable. In this case it must seem to you that to part with them would be an impiety of the worst kind, a simple sacrilege!"

Miss Tita shook her head, full of her dolefulness. "You would understand if you had known her. I'm afraid," she quavered suddenly—"I'm afraid! She was terrible when she was angry."

"Yes, I saw something of that, that night. She was terrible. Then I saw her eyes. Lord, they were fine!"

"I see them—they stare at me in the dark!" said Miss Tita.

"You are nervous, with all you have been through."

"Oh, yes, very—very!"

"You mustn't mind; that will pass away," I said, kindly. Then I added, resignedly, for it really seemed to me that I must accept the situation, "Well, so it is, and it can't be helped. I must renounce." Miss Tita, at this, looking at me, gave a low, soft moan, and I went on: "I only wish to heaven she had destroyed them; then there would be nothing more to say. And I can't understand why, with her ideas, she didn't."

"Oh, she lived on them!" said Miss Tita.

"You can imagine whether that makes me want less to see them," I answered, smiling. "But don't let me stand here as if I had it in my soul to tempt you to do anything base. Naturally you will understand if I give up my rooms. I leave Venice immediately." And I took up my hat, which I had placed on a chair. We were still there rather awkwardly, on our feet, in the middle of the sala. She had left the door of the apartments open behind her but she had not led me that way.

A kind of spasm came into her face as she saw me take my hat. "Immediately—do you mean today?" The tone of the words was tragical—they were a cry of desolation.

"Oh, no; not so long as I can be of the least service to you."

"Well, just a day or two more—just two or three days," she panted. Then controlling herself, she added in another manner, "She wanted to say something to me—the last day—something very particular, but she couldn't."

"Something very particular?"

"Something more about the papers."

"And did you guess—have you any idea?"

"No, I have thought—but I don't know. I have thought all kinds of things."

"And for instance?"

"Well, that if you were a relation it would be different."

"If I were a relation?"

"If you were not a stranger. Then it would be the same for you as for me. Anything that is mine—would be yours, and you could do what you like. I couldn't prevent you—and you would have no responsibility."

She brought out this droll explanation with a little nervous rush, as if she were speaking words she had got by heart. They gave me an impression of subtlety and at first I failed to follow. But after a moment her face helped me to see further, and then a light came into my mind. It was embarrassing, and I bent my head over Jeffrey Aspern's portrait. What an odd expression was in his face! "Get out of it as you can, my dear fellow!" I put the picture into the pocket of my coat and said to Miss Tita, "Yes, I'll sell it for you. I shan't get a thousand pounds by any means, but I shall get something good."

She looked at me with tears in her eyes, but she seemed to try to smile as she remarked, "We can divide the money."

"No, no, it shall be all yours." Then I went on, "I think I know what your poor aunt wanted to say. She wanted to give directions that her papers should be buried with her."

Miss Tita appeared to consider this suggestion for a moment; after which she declared, with striking decision, “Oh no, she wouldn’t have thought that safe!”

“It seems to me nothing could be safer.”

“She had an idea that when people want to publish they are capable—” And she paused, blushing.

“Of violating a tomb? Mercy on us, what must she have thought of me!”

“She was not just, she was not generous!” Miss Tita cried with sudden passion.

The light that had come into my mind a moment before increased. “Ah, don’t say that, for we ARE a dreadful race.” Then I pursued, “If she left a will, that may give you some idea.”

“I have found nothing of the sort—she destroyed it. She was very fond of me,” Miss Tita added incongruously. “She wanted me to be happy. And if any person should be kind to me—she wanted to speak of that.”

I was almost awestricken at the astuteness with which the good lady found herself inspired, transparent astuteness as it was and sewn, as the phrase is, with white thread. “Depend upon it she didn’t want to make any provision that would be agreeable to me.”

“No, not to you but to me. She knew I should like it if you could carry out your idea. Not because she cared for you but because she did think of me,” Miss Tita went on with her unexpected, persuasive volubility. “You could see them—you could use them.” She stopped, seeing that I perceived the sense of that conditional—stopped long enough for me to give some sign which I did not give. She must have been conscious, however, that though my face showed the greatest embarrassment that was ever painted on a human countenance it was not set as a stone, it was also full of compassion. It was a comfort to me a long time afterward to consider that she could not have seen in me the smallest symptom of disrespect. “I don’t know what to do; I’m too tormented, I’m too ashamed!” she continued with vehemence. Then turning away from me and burying her face in her hands she burst into a flood of tears. If she did not know what to do it may be imagined whether I did any better. I stood there dumb, watching her while her sobs resounded in the great empty hall. In a moment she was facing me again, with her streaming eyes. "I would give you everything—and she would understand, where she is—she would forgive me!"

"Ah, Miss Tita—ah, Miss Tita," I stammered, for all reply. I did not know what to do, as I say, but at a venture I made a wild, vague movement in consequence of which I found myself at the door. I remember standing there and saying, "It wouldn't do—it wouldn't do!" pensively, awkwardly, grotesquely, while I looked away to the opposite end of the sala as if there were a beautiful view there. The next thing I remember is that I was downstairs and out of the house. My gondola was there and my gondolier, reclining on the cushions, sprang up as soon as he saw me. I jumped in and to his usual "Dove commanda?" I replied, in a tone that made him stare, "Anywhere, anywhere; out into the lagoon!"

He rowed me away and I sat there prostrate, groaning softly to myself, with my hat pulled over my face. What in the name of the preposterous did she mean if she did not mean to offer me her hand? That was the price—that was the price! And did she think I wanted it, poor deluded, infatuated, extravagant lady? My gondolier, behind me, must have seen my ears red as I wondered, sitting there under the fluttering tenda, with my hidden face, noticing nothing as we passed—wondered whether her delusion, her infatuation had been my own reckless work. Did she think I had made love to her, even to get the papers? I had not, I had not; I repeated that over to myself for an hour, for two hours, till I was wearied if not convinced. I don't know where my gondolier took me; we floated aimlessly about in the lagoon, with slow, rare strokes. At last I became conscious that we were near the Lido, far up, on the right hand, as you turn your back to Venice, and I made him put me ashore. I wanted to walk, to move, to shed some of my bewilderment. I crossed the narrow strip and got to the sea beach—I took my way toward Malamocco. But presently I flung myself down again on the warm sand, in the breeze, on the coarse dry grass. It took it out of me to think I had been so much at fault, that I had unwittingly but nonetheless deplorably trifled. But I had not given her cause—distinctly I had not. I had said to Mrs. Prest that I would make love to her; but it had been a joke without consequences and I had never said it to Tita Bordereau. I had been as kind as possible, because I really liked her; but since when had that become a crime where a woman of such an age and such an appearance was concerned? I am far from remembering clearly the succession of events and feelings during this long day of confusion, which I spent entirely in wandering about, without going home, until late at night; it only comes back to me that there were moments when I pacified my conscience and others when I lashed it into pain. I did not laugh all day—that I do recollect; the case, however it might have struck others, seemed to me so little amusing. It would have been better perhaps for me to feel the comic side of it. At any rate, whether I had given cause or not it went without saying that I could not pay the price. I could not accept. I could not, for a bundle of tattered papers, marry a ridiculous, pathetic, provincial old woman. It was a proof that she did not think the idea would come to me, her having determined to suggest it herself in that practical, argumentative, heroic way, in which the timidity however had been so much more striking than the boldness that her reasons appeared to come first and her feelings afterward.

As the day went on I grew to wish that I had never heard of Aspern's relics, and I cursed the extravagant curiosity that had put John Cumnor on the scent of them. We had more than enough material without them, and my predicament was the just punishment of that most fatal of human follies, our not having known when to stop. It was very well to say it was no predicament, that the way out was simple, that I had only to leave Venice by the first train in the morning, after writing a note to Miss Tita, to be placed in her hand as soon as I got clear of the house; for it was a strong sign that I was embarrassed that when I tried to make up the note in my mind in advance (I would put it on paper as soon as I got home, before going to bed), I could not think of anything but "How can I thank you for the rare confidence you have placed in me?" That would never do; it sounded exactly as if an acceptance were to follow. Of course I might go away without writing a word, but that would be brutal and my idea was still to exclude brutal solutions. As my confusion cooled I was lost in wonder at the importance I had attached to Miss Bordereau's crumpled scraps; the thought of them became odious to me, and I was as vexed with the old witch for the superstition that had prevented her from destroying them as I was with myself for having already spent more money than I could afford in attempting to control their fate. I forget what I did, where I went after leaving the Lido and at what hour or with what recovery of composure I made my way back to my boat. I only know that in the afternoon, when the air was aglow with the sunset, I was standing before the church of Saints John and Paul and looking up at the small square-jawed face of Bartolommeo Colleoni, the terrible condottiere who sits so sturdily astride of his huge bronze horse, on the high pedestal on which Venetian gratitude maintains him. The statue is incomparable, the finest of all mounted figures, unless that of Marcus Aurelius, who rides benignant before the Roman Capitol, be finer: but I was not thinking of that; I only found myself staring at the triumphant captain as if he had an oracle on his lips. The western light shines into all his grimness at that hour and makes it wonderfully personal. But he continued to look far over my head, at the red immersion of another day—he had seen so many go down into the lagoon through the centuries—and if he were thinking of battles and stratagems they were of a different quality from any I had to tell him of. He could not direct me what to do, gaze up at him as I might. Was it before this or after that I wandered about for an hour in the small canals, to the continued stupefaction of my gondolier, who had never seen me so restless and yet so void of a purpose and could extract from me no order but "Go anywhere—everywhere—all over the place"? He reminded me that I had not lunched and expressed therefore respectfully the hope that I would dine earlier. He had had long periods of leisure during the day, when I had left the boat and rambled, so that I was not obliged to consider him, and I told him that that day, for a change, I would touch no meat. It was an effect of poor Miss Tita's proposal, not altogether auspicious, that I had quite lost my appetite. I don't know why it happened that on this occasion I was more than ever struck with that queer air of sociability, of cousinship and family life, which makes up half the expression of Venice. Without streets and vehicles, the uproar of wheels, the brutality of horses, and with its little winding ways where people crowd together, where voices sound as in the corridors of a house, where the human step circulates as if it skirted the angles of furniture and shoes never wear out, the place has the character of an immense collective apartment, in which Piazza San Marco is the most ornamented corner and palaces and churches, for the rest, play the part of great divans of repose, tables of entertainment, expanses of decoration. And somehow the splendid common domicile, familiar, domestic, and resonant, also resembles a theater, with actors clicking over bridges and, in straggling processions, tripping along fondamentas. As you sit in your gondola the footways that in certain parts edge the canals assume to the eye the importance of a stage, meeting it at the same angle, and the Venetian figures, moving to and fro against the battered scenery of their little houses of comedy, strike you as members of an endless dramatic troupe.

I went to bed that night very tired, without being able to compose a letter to Miss Tita. Was this failure the reason why I became conscious the next morning as soon as I awoke of a determination to see the poor lady again the first moment she would receive me? That had something to do with it, but what had still more was the fact that during my sleep a very odd revulsion had taken place in my spirit. I found myself aware of this almost as soon as I opened my eyes; it made me jump out of my bed with the movement of a man who remembers that he has left the house door ajar or a candle burning under a shelf. Was I still in time to save my goods? That question was in my heart; for what had now come to pass was that in the unconscious cerebration of sleep I had swung back to a passionate appreciation of Miss Bordereau's papers. They were now more precious than ever, and a kind of ferocity had come into my desire to possess them. The condition Miss Tita had attached to the possession of them no longer appeared an obstacle worth thinking of, and for an hour, that morning, my repentant imagination brushed it aside. It was absurd that I should be able to invent nothing; absurd to renounce so easily and turn away helpless from the idea that the only way to get hold of the papers was to unite myself to her for life. I would not unite myself and yet I would have them. I must add that by the time I sent down to ask if she would see me I had invented no alternative, though to do so I had had all the time that I was dressing. This failure was humiliating, yet what could the alternative be? Miss Tita sent back word that I might come; and as I descended the stairs and crossed the sala to her door—this time she received me in her aunt's forlorn parlor—I hoped she would not think my errand was to tell her I accepted her hand. She certainly would have made the day before the reflection that I declined it.

As soon as I came into the room I saw that she had drawn this inference, but I also saw something which had not been in my forecast. Poor Miss Tita's sense of her failure had produced an extraordinary alteration in her, but I had been too full of my literary concupiscence to think of that. Now I perceived it; I can scarcely tell how it startled me. She stood in the middle of the room with a face of mildness bent upon me, and her look of forgiveness, of absolution, made her angelic. It beautified her; she was younger; she was not a ridiculous old woman. This optical trick gave her a sort of phantasmagoric brightness, and while I was still the victim of it I heard a whisper somewhere in the depths of my conscience: "Why not, after all—why not?" It seemed to me I was ready to pay the price. Still more distinctly however than the whisper I heard Miss Tita's own voice. I was so struck with the different effect she made upon me that at first I was not clearly aware of what she was saying; then I perceived she had bade me goodbye—she said something about hoping I should be very happy.

"Goodbye—goodbye?" I repeated with an inflection interrogative and probably foolish.

I saw she did not feel the interrogation, she only heard the words; she had strung herself up to accepting our separation and they fell upon her ear as a proof. "Are you going today?" she asked. "But it doesn't matter, for whenever you go I shall not see you again. I don't want to." And she smiled strangely, with an infinite gentleness. She had never doubted that I had left her the day before in horror. How could she, since I had not come back before night to contradict, even as a simple form, such an idea? And now she had the force of soul—Miss Tita with force of soul was a new conception—to smile at me in her humiliation.

"What shall you do—where shall you go?" I asked.

"Oh, I don't know. I have done the great thing. I have destroyed the papers."

"Destroyed them?" I faltered.

"Yes; what was I to keep them for? I burned them last night, one by one, in the kitchen."

"One by one?" I repeated, mechanically.

"It took a long time—there were so many." The room seemed to go round me as she said this, and a real darkness for a moment descended upon my eyes. When it passed Miss Tita was there still, but the transfiguration was over and she had changed back to a plain, dingy, elderly person. It was in this character she spoke as she said, "I can't stay with you longer, I can't;" and it was in this character that she turned her back upon me, as I had turned mine upon her twenty-four hours before, and moved to the door of her room. Here she did what I had not done when I quitted her—she paused long enough to give me one look. I have never forgotten it and I sometimes still suffer from it, though it was not resentful. No, there was no resentment, nothing hard or vindictive in poor Miss Tita; for when, later, I sent her in exchange for the portrait of Jeffrey Aspern a larger sum of money than I had hoped to be able to gather for her, writing to her that I had sold the picture, she kept it with thanks; she never sent it back. I wrote to her that I had sold the picture, but I admitted to Mrs. Prest, at the time (I met her in London, in the autumn), that it hangs above my writing table. When I look at it my chagrin at the loss of the letters becomes almost intolerable.

THE AUTHOR OF BELTRAFFIO

I

Much as I wished to see him I had kept my letter of introduction three weeks in my pocket-book. I was nervous and timid about meeting him—conscious of youth and ignorance, convinced that he was tormented by strangers, and especially by my country-people, and not exempt from the suspicion that he had the irritability as well as the dignity of genius. Moreover, the pleasure, if it should occur—for I could scarcely believe it was near at hand—would be so great that I wished to think of it in advance, to feel it there against my breast, not to mix it with satisfactions more superficial and usual. In the little game of new sensations that I was playing with my ingenuous mind I wished to keep my visit to the author of "Beltraffio" as a trump-card. It was three years after the publication of that fascinating work, which I had read over five times and which now, with my riper judgement, I admire on the whole as much as ever. This will give you about the date of my first visit—of any duration—to England for you will not have forgotten the commotion, I may even say the scandal, produced by Mark Ambient's masterpiece. It was the most complete presentation that had yet been made of the gospel of art; it was a kind of æsthetic war-cry. People had endeavoured to sail nearer to "truth" in the cut of their sleeves and the shape of their sideboards; but there had not as yet been, among English novels, such an example of beauty of execution and "intimate" importance of theme. Nothing had been done in that line from the point of view of art for art. That served me as a fond formula, I may mention, when I was twenty-five; how much it still serves I won't take upon myself to say—especially as the discerning reader will be able to judge for himself. I had been in England, briefly, a twelve-month before the time to which I began by alluding, and had then learned that Mr. Ambient was in distant lands—was making a considerable tour in the East; so that there was nothing to do but to keep my letter till I should be in London again. It was of little use to me to hear that his wife had not left England and was, with her little boy, their only child, spending the period of her husband's absence—a good many months—at a small place they had down in Surrey. They had a house in London, but actually in the occupation of other persons. All this I had picked up, and also that Mrs. Ambient was charming—my friend the American poet, from whom I had my introduction, had never seen her, his relations with the great man confined to the exchange of letters; but she wasn't, after all, though she had lived so near the rose, the author of "Beltraffio," and I didn't go down into Surrey to call on her. I went to the Continent, spent the following winter in Italy, and returned to London in May. My visit to Italy had opened my eyes to a good many things, but to nothing more than the beauty of certain pages in the works of Mark Ambient. I carried his productions about in my trunk—they are not, as you know, very numerous, but he had preluded to "Beltraffio" by, some exquisite things—and I used to read them over in the evening at the inn. I used profoundly to reason that the man who drew those characters and wrote that style understood what he saw and knew what he was doing. This is my sole ground for mentioning my winter in Italy. He had been there much in former years—he was saturated with what painters call the "feeling" of that classic land. He expressed the charm of the old hill-cities of Tuscany, the look of certain lonely grass-grown places which, in the past, had echoed with life; he understood the great artists, he understood the spirit of the Renaissance; he understood everything. The scene of one of his earlier novels was laid in Rome, the scene of another in Florence, and I had moved through these cities in company with the figures he set so firmly on their feet. This is why I was now so much happier even than before in the prospect of making his acquaintance.

At last, when I had dallied with my privilege long enough, I despatched to him the missive of the American poet. He had already gone out of town; he shrank from the rigour of the London "season" and it was his habit to migrate on the first of June. Moreover I had heard he was this year hard at work on a new book, into which some of his impressions of the East were to be wrought, so that he desired nothing so much as quiet days. That knowledge, however, didn't prevent me—*cet âge est sans pitié*—from sending with my friend's letter a note of my own, in which I asked his leave to come down and see him for an hour or two on some day to be named by himself. My proposal was accompanied with a very frank expression of my sentiments, and the effect of the entire appeal was to elicit from the great man the kindest possible invitation. He would be delighted to see me, especially if I should turn up on the following Saturday and would remain till the Monday morning. We would take a walk over the Surrey commons, and I could tell him all about the other great man, the one in America. He indicated to me the best train, and it may be imagined whether on the Saturday afternoon I was punctual at Waterloo. He carried his benevolence to the point of coming to meet me at the little station at which I was to alight, and my heart beat very fast as I saw his handsome face, surmounted with a soft wide-awake and which I knew by a photograph long since enshrined on my mantel-shelf, scanning the carriage-windows as the train rolled up. He recognised me as infallibly as I had recognised himself; he appeared to know by instinct how a young American of critical pretensions, rash youth, would look when much divided between eagerness and modesty. He took me by the hand and smiled at me and said: "You must be—a—*you*, I think!" and asked if I should mind going on foot to his house, which would take but a few minutes. I remember feeling it a piece of extraordinary affability that he should give directions about the conveyance of my bag; I remember feeling altogether very happy and rosy, in fact quite transported, when he laid his hand on my shoulder as we came out of the station.

I surveyed him, askance, as we walked together; I had already, I had indeed instantly, seen him as all delightful. His face is so well known that I needn't describe it; he looked to me at once an English gentleman and a man of genius, and I thought that a happy combination. There was a brush of the Bohemian in his fineness; you would easily have guessed his belonging to the artist guild. He was addicted to velvet jackets, to cigarettes, to loose shirt-collars, to looking a little dishevelled. His features, which were firm but not perfectly regular, are fairly enough represented in his portraits; but no portrait I have seen gives any idea of his expression. There were innumerable things in it, and they chased each other in and out of his face. I have seen people who were grave and gay in quick alternation; but Mark Ambient was grave and gay at one and the same moment. There were other strange oppositions and contradictions in his slightly faded and fatigued countenance. He affected me somehow as at once fresh and stale, at once anxious and indifferent. He had evidently had an active past, which inspired one with curiosity; yet what was that compared to his obvious future? He was just enough above middle height to be spoken of as tall, and rather lean and long in the flank. He had the friendliest frankest manner possible, and yet I could see it cost him something. It cost him small spasms of the self-consciousness that is an Englishman's last and dearest treasure—the thing he pays his way through life by sacrificing small pieces of even as the gallant but moneyless adventurer in "Quentin Durward" broke off links of his brave gold chain. He had been thirty-eight years old at the time "Beltraffio" was published. He asked me about his friend in America, about the length of my stay in England, about the last news in London and the people I had seen there; and I remember looking for the signs of genius in the very form of his questions and thinking I found it. I liked his voice as if I were somehow myself having the use of it.

There was genius in his house too I thought when we got there; there was imagination in the carpets and curtains, in the pictures and books, in the garden behind it, where certain old brown walls were muffled in creepers that appeared to me to have been copied from a masterpiece of one of the pre-Raphaelites. That was the way many things struck me at that time, in England—as reproductions of something that existed primarily in art or literature. It was not the picture, the poem, the fictive page, that seemed to me a copy; these things were the originals, and the life of happy and distinguished people was fashioned in their image. Mark Ambient called his house a cottage, and I saw afterwards he was right for if it hadn't been a cottage it must have been a villa, and a villa, in England at least, was not a place in which one could fancy him at home. But it was, to my vision, a cottage glorified and translated; it was a palace of art, on a slightly reduced scale—and might besides have been the dearest haunt of the old English *genius loci.* It nestled under a cluster of magnificent beeches, it had little creaking lattices that opened out of, or into, pendent mats of ivy, and gables, and old red tiles, as well as a general aspect of being painted in water-colours and inhabited by people whose lives would go on in chapters and volumes. The lawn seemed to me of extraordinary extent, the garden-walls of incalculable height, the whole air of the place delightfully still, private, proper to itself. "My wife must be somewhere about," Mark Ambient said as we went in. "We shall find her perhaps—we've about an hour before dinner. She may be in the garden. I'll show you my little place."

We passed through the house and into the grounds, as I should have called them, which extended into the rear. They covered scarce three or four acres, but, like the house, were very old and crooked and full of traces of long habitation, with inequalities of level and little flights of steps—mossy and cracked were these—which connected the different parts with each other. The limits of the place, cleverly dissimulated, were muffled in the great verdurous screens. They formed, as I remember, a thick loose curtain at the further end, in one of the folds of which, as it were, we presently made out from afar a little group. "Ah there she is!" said Mark Ambient; "and she has got the boy." He noted that last fact in a slightly different tone from any in which he yet had spoken. I wasn't fully aware of this at the time, but it lingered in my ear and I afterwards understood it.

"Is it your son?" I inquired, feeling the question not to be brilliant.

"Yes, my only child. He's always in his mother's pocket. She coddles him too much." It came back to me afterwards too—the sound of these critical words. They weren't petulant; they expressed rather a sudden coldness, a mechanical submission. We went a few steps further, and then he stopped short and called the boy, beckoning to him repeatedly.

"Dolcino, come and see your daddy!" There was something in the way he stood still and waited that made me think he did it for a purpose. Mrs. Ambient had her arm round the child's waist, and he was leaning against her knee; but though he moved at his father's call she gave no sign of releasing him. A lady, apparently a neighbour, was seated near her, and before them was a garden-table on which a tea-service had been placed.

Mark Ambient called again, and Dolcino struggled in the maternal embrace; but, too tightly held, he after two or three fruitless efforts jerked about and buried his head deep in his mother's lap. There was a certain awkwardness in the scene; I thought it odd Mrs. Ambient should pay so little attention to her husband. But I wouldn't for the world have betrayed my thought, and, to conceal it, I began loudly to rejoice in the prospect of our having tea in the garden. "Ah she won't let him come!" said my host with a sigh; and we went our way till we reached the two ladies. He mentioned my name to his wife, and I noticed that he addressed her as "My dear," very genially, without a trace of resentment at her detention of the child. The quickness of the transition made me vaguely ask myself if he were perchance henpecked—a shocking surmise which I instantly dismissed. Mrs. Ambient was quite such a wife as I should have expected him to have; slim and fair, with a long neck and pretty eyes and an air of good breeding. She shone with a certain coldness and practised in intercourse a certain bland detachment, but she was clothed in gentleness as in one of those vaporous redundant scarves that muffle the heroines of Gainsborough and Romney. She had also a vague air of race, justified by my afterwards learning that she was "connected with the aristocracy." I have seen poets married to women of whom it was difficult to conceive that they should gratify the poetic fancy—women with dull faces and glutinous minds, who were none the less, however, excellent wives. But there was no obvious disparity in Mark Ambient's union. My hostess—so far as she could be called so—delicate and quiet, in a white dress, with her beautiful child at her side, was worthy of the author of a work so distinguished as "Beltraffio." Round her neck she wore a black velvet ribbon, of which the long ends, tied behind, hung down her back, and to which, in front, was attached a miniature portrait of her little boy. Her smooth shining hair was confined in a net. She gave me an adequate greeting, and Dolcino—I thought this small name of endearment delightful—took advantage of her getting up to slip away from her and go to his father, who seized him in silence and held him high for a long moment, kissing him several times.

I had lost no time in observing that the child, not more than seven years old, was extraordinarily beautiful. He had the face of an angel—the eyes, the hair, the smile of innocence, the more than mortal bloom. There was something that deeply touched, that almost alarmed, in his beauty, composed, one would have said, of elements too fine and pure for the breath of this world. When I spoke to him and he came and held out his hand and smiled at me I felt a sudden strange pity for him—quite as if he had been an orphan or a changeling or stamped with some social stigma. It was impossible to be in fact more exempt from these misfortunes, and yet, as one kissed him, it was hard to keep from murmuring all tenderly "Poor little devil!" though why one should have applied this epithet to a living cherub is more than I can say. Afterwards indeed I knew a trifle better; I grasped the truth of his being too fair to live, wondering at the same time that his parents shouldn't have guessed it and have been in proportionate grief and despair. For myself I had no doubt of his evanescence, having already more than once caught in the fact the particular infant charm that's as good as a death-warrant.

The lady who had been sitting with Mrs. Ambient was a jolly ruddy personage in velveteen and limp feathers, whom I guessed to be the vicar's wife—our hostess didn't introduce me—and who immediately began to talk to Ambient about chrysanthemums. This was a safe subject, and yet there was a certain surprise for me in seeing the author of "Beltraffio" even in such superficial communion with the Church of England. His writings implied so much detachment from that institution, expressed a view of life so profane, as it were, so independent and so little likely in general to be thought edifying, that I should have expected to find him an object of horror to vicars and their ladies—of horror repaid on his own part by any amount of effortless derision. This proved how little I knew as yet of the English people and their extraordinary talent for keeping up their forms, as well as of some of the mysteries of Mark Ambient's hearth and home. I found afterwards that he had, in his study, between nervous laughs and free cigar-puffs, some wonderful comparisons for his clerical neighbours; but meanwhile the chrysanthemums were a source of harmony, he and the vicaress were equally attached to them, and I was surprised at the knowledge they exhibited of this interesting plant. The lady's visit, however, had presumably been long, and she presently rose for departure and kissed Mrs. Ambient. Mark started to walk with her to the gate of the grounds, holding Dolcino by the hand.

"Stay with me, darling," Mrs. Ambient said to the boy, who had surrendered himself to his father.

Mark paid no attention to the summons but Dolcino turned and looked at her in shy appeal, "Can't I go with papa?"

"Not when I ask you to stay with me."

"But please don't ask me, mamma," said the child in his small clear new voice.

"I must ask you when I want you. Come to me, dearest." And Mrs. Ambient, who had seated herself again, held out her long slender slightly too osseous hands.

Her husband stopped, his back turned to her, but without releasing the child. He was still talking to the vicaress, but this good lady, I think, had lost the thread of her attention. She looked at Mrs. Ambient and at Dolcino, and then looked at me, smiling in a highly amused cheerful manner and almost to a grimace.

"Papa," said the child, "mamma wants me not to go with you."

"He's very tired—he has run about all day. He ought to be quiet till he goes to bed. Otherwise he won't sleep." These declarations fell successively and very distinctly from Mrs. Ambient's lips.

Her husband, still without turning round, bent over the boy and looked at him in silence. The vicaress gave a genial irrelevant laugh and observed that he was a precious little pet. "Let him choose," said Mark Ambient. "My dear little boy, will you go with me or will you stay with your mother?"

"Oh it's a shame!" cried the vicar's lady with increased hilarity.

"Papa, I don't think I can choose," the child answered, making his voice very low and confidential. "But I've been a great deal with mamma to-day," he then added.

"And very little with papa! My dear fellow, I think you *have* chosen!" On which Mark Ambient walked off with his son, accompanied by re-echoing but inarticulate comments from my fellow-visitor.

His wife had seated herself again, and her fixed eyes, bent on the ground, expressed for a few moments so much mute agitation that anything I could think of to say would be but a false note. Yet she none the less quickly recovered herself, to express the sufficiently civil hope that I didn't mind having had to walk from the station. I reassured her on this point, and she went on: “We’ve got a thing that might have gone for you, but my husband wouldn’t order it.” After which and another longish pause, broken only by my plea that the pleasure of a walk with our friend would have been quite what I would have chosen, she found for reply: “I believe the Americans walk very little.”

“Yes, we always run,” I laughingly allowed.

She looked at me seriously, yet with an absence in her pretty eyes. “I suppose your distances are so great.”

“Yes, but we break our marches! I can’t tell you the pleasure to me of finding myself here,” I added. “I’ve the greatest admiration for Mr. Ambient.”

“He’ll like that. He likes being admired.”

“He must have a very happy life, then. He has many worshippers.”

“Oh yes, I’ve seen some of them,” she dropped, looking away, very far from me, rather as if such a vision were before her at the moment. It seemed to indicate, her tone, that the sight was scarcely edifying, and I guessed her quickly enough to be in no great intellectual sympathy with the author of “Beltraffio.” I thought the fact strange, but somehow, in the glow of my own enthusiasm, didn’t think it important it only made me wish rather to emphasise that homage.

“For me, you know,” I returned—doubtless with a due *suffisance*—“he’s quite the greatest of living writers.”

“Of course I can’t judge. Of course he’s very clever,” she said with a patient cheer.

“He’s nothing less than supreme, Mrs. Ambient! There are pages in each of his books of a perfection classing them with the greatest things. Accordingly for me to see him in this familiar way, in his habit as he lives, and apparently to find the man as delightful as the artist—well, I can’t tell you how much too good to be true it seems and how great a privilege I think it.” I knew I was gushing, but I couldn’t help it, and what I said was a good deal less than what I felt. I was by no means sure I should dare to say even so much as this to the master himself, and there was a kind of rapture in speaking it out to his wife which was not affected by the fact that, as a wife, she appeared peculiar. She listened to me with her face grave again and her lips a little compressed, listened as if in no doubt, of course, that her husband was remarkable, but as if at the same time she had heard it frequently enough and couldn't treat it as stirring news. There was even in her manner a suggestion that I was so young as to expose myself to being called forward—an imputation and a word I had always loathed; as well as a hinted reminder that people usually got over their early extravagance. "I assure you that for me this is a red-letter day," I added.

She didn't take this up, but after a pause, looking round her, said abruptly and a trifle dryly: "We're very much afraid about the fruit this year."

My eyes wandered to the mossy mottled garden-walls, where plum-trees and pears, flattened and fastened upon the rusty bricks, looked like crucified figures with many arms. "Doesn't it promise well?"

"No, the trees look very dull. We had such late frosts."

Then there was another pause. She addressed her attention to the opposite end of the grounds, kept it for her husband's return with the child. "Is Mr. Ambient fond of gardening?" it occurred to me to ask, irresistibly impelled as I felt myself, moreover, to bring the conversation constantly back to him.

"He's very fond of plums," said his wife.

"Ah well, then, I hope your crop will be better than you fear. It's a lovely old place," I continued. "The whole impression's that of certain places he has described. Your house is like one of his pictures."

She seemed a bit frigidly amused at my glow. "It's a pleasant little place. There are hundreds like it."

"Oh it has his *tone*," I laughed, but sounding my epithet and insisting on my point the more sharply that my companion appeared to see in my appreciation of her simple establishment a mark of mean experience.

It was clear I insisted too much. "His tone?" she repeated with a harder look at me and a slightly heightened colour.

"Surely he has a tone, Mrs. Ambient."

"Oh yes, he has indeed! But I don't in the least consider that I'm living in one of his books at all. I shouldn't care for that in the least," she went on with a smile that had in some degree the effect of converting her really sharp protest into an insincere joke. "I'm afraid I'm not very literary. And I'm not artistic," she stated.

"I'm very sure you're not ignorant, not stupid," I ventured to reply, with the accompaniment of feeling immediately afterwards that I had been both familiar and patronising. My only consolation was in the sense that she had begun it, had fairly dragged me into it. She had thrust forward her limitations.

"Well, whatever I am I'm very different from my husband. If you like him you won't like me. You needn't say anything. Your liking me isn't in the least necessary!"

"Don't defy me!" I could but honourably make answer.

She looked as if she hadn't heard me, which was the best thing she could do; and we sat some time without further speech. Mrs. Ambient had evidently the enviable English quality of being able to be mute without unrest. But at last she spoke—she asked me if there seemed many people in town. I gave her what satisfaction I could on this point, and we talked a little of London and of some of its characteristics at that time of the year. At the end of this I came back irrepressibly to Mark.

"Doesn't he like to be there now? I suppose he doesn't find the proper quiet for his work. I should think his things had been written for the most part in a very still place. They suggest a great stillness following on a kind of tumult. Don't you think so?" I laboured on. "I suppose London's a tremendous place to collect impressions, but a refuge like this, in the country, must be better for working them up. Does he get many of his impressions in London, should you say?" I proceeded from point to point in this malign inquiry simply because my hostess, who probably thought me an odious chattering person, gave me time; for when I paused—I've not represented my pauses—she simply continued to let her eyes wander while her long fair fingers played with the medallion on her neck. When I stopped altogether, however, she was obliged to say something, and what she said was that she hadn't the least idea where her husband got his impressions. This made me think her, for a moment, positively disagreeable; delicate and proper and rather aristocratically fine as she sat there. But I must either have lost that view a moment later or been goaded by it to further aggression, for I remember asking her if our great man were in a good vein of work and when we might look for the appearance of the book on which he was engaged. I've every reason now to know that she found me insufferable.

She gave a strange small laugh as she said: "I'm afraid you think I know much more about my husband's work than I do. I haven't the least idea what he's doing," she then added in a slightly different, that is a more explanatory, tone and as if from a glimpse of the enormity of her confession. "I don't read what he writes."

She didn't succeed, and wouldn't even had she tried much harder, in making this seem to me anything less than monstrous. I stared at her and I think I blushed. "Don't you admire his genius? Don't you admire 'Beltraffio'?"

She waited, and I wondered what she could possibly say. She didn't speak, I could see, the first words that rose to her lips; she repeated what she had said a few minutes before. "Oh of course he's very clever!" And with this she got up; our two absentees had reappeared.

II

Mrs. Ambient left me and went to meet them; she stopped and had a few words with her husband that I didn't hear and that ended in her taking the child by the hand and returning with him to the house. Her husband joined me in a moment, looking, I thought, the least bit conscious and constrained, and said that if I would come in with him he would show me my room. In looking back upon these first moments of my visit I find it important to avoid the error of appearing to have at all fully measured his situation from the first or made out the signs of things mastered only afterwards. This later knowledge throws a backward light and makes me forget that, at least on the occasion of my present reference—I mean that first afternoon—Mark Ambient struck me as only enviable. Allowing for this he must yet have failed of much expression as we walked back to the house, though I remember well the answer he made to a remark of mine on his small son.

"That's an extraordinary little boy of yours. I've never seen such a child."

"Why," he asked while we went, "do you call him extraordinary?"

"He's so beautiful, so fascinating. He's like some perfect little work of art."

He turned quickly in the passage, grasping my arm. "Oh don't call him that, or you'll—you'll—!"

But in his hesitation he broke off suddenly, laughing at my surprise. Immediately afterwards, however, he added: "You'll make his little future very difficult."

I declared that I wouldn't for the world take any liberties with his little future—it seemed to me to hang by threads of such delicacy. I should only be highly interested in watching it.

"You Americans are very keen," he commented on this. "You notice more things than we do."

"Ah if you want visitors who aren't struck with you," I cried, "you shouldn't have asked me down here!"

He showed me my room, a little bower of chintz, with open windows where the light was green, and before he left me said irrelevantly: "As for my small son, you know, we shall probably kill him between us before we've done with him!" And he made this assertion as if he really believed it, without any appearance of jest, his fine near-sighted expressive eyes looking straight into mine.

"Do you mean by spoiling him?"

"No, by fighting for him!"

"You had better give him to me to keep for you," I said. "Let me remove the apple of discord!"

It was my extravagance of course, but he had the air of being perfectly serious. "It would be quite the best thing we could do. I should be all ready to do it."

"I'm greatly obliged to you for your confidence."

But he lingered with his hands in his pockets. I felt as if within a few moments I had, morally speaking, taken several steps nearer to him. He looked weary, just as he faced me then, looked preoccupied and as if there were something one might do for him. I was terribly conscious of the limits of my young ability, but I wondered what such a service might be, feeling at bottom nevertheless that the only thing I could do for him was to like him. I suppose he guessed this and was grateful for what was in my mind, since he went on presently: "I haven't the advantage of being an American, but I also notice a little, and I've an idea that"—here he smiled and laid his hand on my shoulder—"even counting out your nationality you're not destitute of intelligence. I've only known you half an hour, but—!" For which again he pulled up. "You're very young, after all."

"But you may treat me as if I could understand you!" I said; and before he left me to dress for dinner he had virtually given me a promise that he would.

When I went down into the drawing-room—I was very punctual—I found that neither my hostess nor my host had appeared. A lady rose from a sofa, however, and inclined her head as I rather surprisedly gazed at her. "I daresay you don't know me," she said with the modern laugh. "I'm Mark Ambient's sister." Whereupon I shook hands with her, saluting her very low. Her laugh was modern—by which I mean that it consisted of the vocal agitation serving between people who meet in drawing-rooms as the solvent of social disparities, the medium of transitions; but her appearance was—what shall I call it?—medieval. She was pale and angular, her long thin face was inhabited by sad dark eyes and her black hair intertwined with golden fillets and curious clasps. She wore a faded velvet robe which clung to her when she moved and was "cut," as to the neck and sleeves, like the garments of old Italians. She suggested a symbolic picture, something akin even to Dürer's Melancholia, and was so perfect an image of a type which I, in my ignorance, supposed to be extinct, that while she rose before me I was almost as much startled as if I had seen a ghost. I afterwards concluded that Miss Ambient wasn't incapable of deriving pleasure from this weird effect, and I now believe that reflexion concerned in her having sunk again to her seat with her long lean but not ungraceful arms locked together in an archaic manner on her knees and her mournful eyes addressing me a message of intentness which foreshadowed what I was subsequently to suffer. She was a singular fatuous artificial creature, and I was never more than half to penetrate her motives and mysteries. Of one thing I'm sure at least: that they were considerably less insuperable than her appearance announced. Miss Ambient was a restless romantic disappointed spinster, consumed with the love of Michael-Angelesque attitudes and mystical robes; but I'm now convinced she hadn't in her nature those depths of unutterable thought which, when you first knew her, seemed to look out from her eyes and to prompt her complicated gestures. Those features in especial had a misleading eloquence; they lingered on you with a far-off dimness, an air of obstructed sympathy, which was certainly not always a key to the spirit of their owner; so that, of a truth, a young lady could scarce have been so dejected and disillusioned without having committed a crime for which she was consumed with remorse, or having parted with a hope that she couldn't sanely have entertained. She had, I believe, the usual allowance of rather vain motives: she wished to be looked at, she wished to be married, she wished to be thought original.

It costs me a pang to speak in this irreverent manner of one of Ambient's name, but I shall have still less gracious things to say before I've finished my anecdote, and moreover—I confess it—I owe the young lady a bit of a grudge. Putting aside the curious cast of her face she had no natural aptitude for an artistic development, had little real intelligence. But her affectations rubbed off on her brother's renown, and as there were plenty of people who darkly disapproved of him they could easily point to his sister as a person formed by his influence. It was quite possible to regard her as a warning, and she had almost compromised him with the world at large. He was the original and she the inevitable imitation. I suppose him scarce aware of the impression she mainly produced, beyond having a general idea that she made up very well as a Rossetti; he was used to her and was sorry for her, wishing she would marry and observing how she didn't. Doubtless I take her too seriously, for she did me no harm, though I'm bound to allow that I can only half-account for her. She wasn't so mystical as she looked, but was a strange indirect uncomfortable embarrassing woman. My story gives the reader at best so very small a knot to untie that I needn't hope to excite his curiosity by delaying to remark that Mrs. Ambient hated her sister-in-law. This I learned but later on, when other matters came to my knowledge. I mention it, however, at once, for I shall perhaps not seem to count too much on having beguiled him if I say he must promptly have guessed it. Mrs. Ambient, a person of conscience, put the best face on her kinswoman, who spent a month with her twice a year; but it took no great insight to recognise the very different personal paste of the two ladies, and that the usual feminine hypocrisies would cost them on either side much more than the usual effort. Mrs. Ambient, smooth-haired, thin-lipped, perpetually fresh, must have regarded her crumpled and dishevelled visitor as an equivocal joke; she herself so the opposite of a Rossetti, she herself a Reynolds or a Lawrence, with no more far-fetched note in her composition than a cold ladylike candour and a well-starched muslin dress.

It was in a garment and with an expression of this kind that she made her entrance after I had exchanged a few words with Miss Ambient. Her husband presently followed her and, there being no other company, we went to dinner. The impressions I received at that repast are present to me still. The elements of oddity in the air hovered, as it were, without descending—to any immediate check of my delight. This came mainly, of course, from Ambient's talk, the easiest and richest I had ever heard. I mayn't say to-day whether he laid himself out to dazzle a rather juvenile pilgrim from over the sea; but that matters little—it seemed so natural to him to shine. His spoken wit or wisdom, or whatever, had thus a charm almost beyond his written; that is if the high finish of his printed prose be really, as some people have maintained, a fault. There was such a kindness in him, however, that I've no doubt it gave him ideas for me, or about me, to see me sit as open-mouthed as I now figure myself. Not so the two ladies, who not only were very nearly dumb from beginning to end of the meal, but who hadn't even the air of being struck with such an exhibition of fancy and taste. Mrs. Ambient, detached, and inscrutable, met neither my eye nor her husband's; she attended to her dinner, watched her servants, arranged the puckers in her dress, exchanged at wide intervals a remark with her sister-in-law and, while she slowly rubbed her lean white hands between the courses, looked out of the window at the first signs of evening—the long June day allowing us to dine without candles. Miss Ambient appeared to give little direct heed to anything said by her brother; but on the other hand she was much engaged in watching its effect upon me. Her "die-away" pupils continued to attach themselves to my countenance, and it was only her air of belonging to another century that kept them from being importunate. She seemed to look at me across the ages, and the interval of time diminished for me the inconvenience. It was as if she knew in a general way that he must be talking very well, but she herself was so at home among such allusions that she had no need to pick them up and was at liberty to see what would become of the exposure of a candid young American to a high æsthetic temperature.

The temperature was æsthetic certainly, but it was less so than I could have desired, for I failed of any great success in making our friend abound about himself. I tried to put him on the ground of his own genius, but he slipped through my fingers every time and shifted the saddle to one or other of his contemporaries. He talked about Balzac and Browning, about what was being done in foreign countries, about his recent tour in the East and the extraordinary forms of life to be observed in that part of the world. I felt he had reasons for holding off from a direct profession of literary faith, a full consistency or sincerity, and therefore dealt instead with certain social topics, treating them with extraordinary humour and with a due play of that power of ironic evocation in which his books abound. He had a deal to say about London as London appears to the observer who has the courage of some of his conclusions during the high-pressure time—from April to July—of its gregarious life. He flashed his faculty of playing with the caught image and liberating the wistful idea over the whole scheme of manners or conception of intercourse of his compatriots, among whom there were evidently not a few types for which he had little love. London in short was grotesque to him, and he made capital sport of it; his only allusion that I can remember to his own work was his saying that he meant some day to do an immense and general, a kind of epic, social satire. Miss Ambient's perpetual gaze seemed to put to me: "Do you perceive how artistic, how very strange and interesting, we are? Frankly now is it possible to be *more* artistic, *more* strange and interesting, than this? You surely won't deny that we're remarkable." I was irritated by her use of the plural pronoun, for she had no right to pair herself with her brother; and moreover, of course, I couldn't see my way to—at all genially—include Mrs. Ambient. Yet there was no doubt they were, taken together, unprecedented enough, and, with all allowances, I had never been left, or condemned, to draw so many rich inferences.

After the ladies had retired my host took me into his study to smoke, where I appealingly brought him round, or so tried, to some disclosure of fond ideals. I was bent on proving I was worthy to listen to him, on repaying him for what he had said to me before dinner, by showing him how perfectly I understood. He liked to talk; he liked to defend his convictions and his honour (not that I attacked them); he liked a little perhaps—it was a pardonable weakness—to bewilder the youthful mind even while wishing to win it over. My ingenuous sympathy received at any rate a shock from three or four of his professions—he made me occasionally gasp and stare. He couldn't help forgetting, or rather couldn't know, how little, in another and drier clime, I had ever sat in the school in which he was master; and he promoted me as at a jump to a sense of its penetralia. My trepidations, however, were delightful; they were just what I had hoped for, and their only fault was that they passed away too quickly; since I found that for the main points I was essentially, I was quite constitutionally, on Mark Ambient's "side." This was the taken stand of the artist to whom every manifestation of human energy was a thrilling spectacle and who felt for ever the desire to resolve his experience of life into a literary form. On that high head of the passion for form the attempt at perfection, the quest for which was to his mind the real search for the holy grail—he said the most interesting, the most inspiring things. He mixed with them a thousand illustrations from his own life, from other lives he had known, from history and fiction, and above all from the annals of the time that was dear to him beyond all periods, the Italian cinquecento. It came to me thus that in his books he had uttered but half his thought, and that what he had kept back from motives I deplored when I made them out later—was the finer and braver part. It was his fate to make a great many still more "prepared" people than me not inconsiderably wince; but there was no grain of bravado in his ripest things (I've always maintained it, though often contradicted), and at bottom the poor fellow, disinterested to his finger-tips and regarding imperfection not only as an æsthetic but quite also as a social crime, had an extreme dread of scandal. There are critics who regret that having gone so far he didn't go further; but I regret nothing—putting aside two or three of the motives I just mentioned—since he arrived at a noble rarity and I don't see how you can go beyond that. The hours I spent in his study—this first one and the few that followed it; they were not, after all, so numerous—seem to glow, as I look back on them, with a tone that is partly that of the brown old room, rich, under the shaded candle-light where we sat and smoked, with the dusky delicate bindings of valuable books; partly that of his voice, of which I still catch the echo, charged with the fancies and figures that came at his command. When we went back to the drawing-room we found Miss Ambient alone in possession and prompt to mention that her sister-in-law had a quarter of an hour before been called by the nurse to see the child, who appeared rather unwell—a little feverish.

"Feverish! how in the world comes he to be feverish?" Ambient asked. "He was perfectly right this afternoon."

"Beatrice says you walked him about too much—you almost killed him."

"Beatrice must be very happy—she has an opportunity to triumph!" said my friend with a bright bitterness which was all I could have wished it.

"Surely not if the child's ill," I ventured to remark by way of pleading for Mrs. Ambient.

"My dear fellow, you aren't married—you don't know the nature of wives!" my host returned with spirit.

I tried to match it. "Possibly not; but I know the nature of mothers."

"Beatrice is perfect as a mother," sighed Miss Ambient quite tremendously and with her fingers interlaced on her embroidered knees.

"I shall go up and see my boy," her brother went on. "Do you suppose he's asleep?"

"Beatrice won't let you see him, dear"—as to which our young lady looked at me, though addressing our companion.

"Do you call that being perfect as a mother?" Ambient asked.

"Yes, from her point of view."

"Damn her point of view!" cried the author of "Beltraffio." And he left the room; after which we heard him ascend the stairs.

I sat there for some ten minutes with Miss Ambient, and we naturally had some exchange of remarks, which began, I think, by my asking her what the point of view of her sister-in-law could be.

"Oh it's so very odd. But we're so very odd altogether. Don't you find us awfully unlike others of our class?—which indeed mostly, in England, is awful. We've lived so much abroad. I adore 'abroad.' Have you people like us in America?"

"You're not all alike, you interesting three—or, counting Dolcino, four—surely, surely; so that I don't think I understand your question. We've no one like your brother—I may go so far as that."

"You've probably more persons like his wife," Miss Ambient desolately smiled.

"I can tell you that better when you've told me about her point of view."

"Oh yes—oh yes. Well," said my entertainer, "she doesn't like his ideas. She doesn't like them for the child. She thinks them undesirable."

Being quite fresh from the contemplation of some of Mark Ambient's *arcana* I was particularly in a position to appreciate this announcement. But the effect of it was to make me, after staring a moment, burst into laughter which I instantly checked when I remembered the indisposed child above and the possibility of parents nervously or fussily anxious.

"What has that infant to do with ideas?" I asked. "Surely he can't tell one from another. Has he read his father's novels?"

"He's very precocious and very sensitive, and his mother thinks she can't begin to guard him too early." Miss Ambient's head drooped a little to one side and her eyes fixed themselves on futurity. Then of a sudden came a strange alteration; her face lighted to an effect more joyless than any gloom, to that indeed of a conscious insincere grimace, and she added "When one has children what one writes becomes a great responsibility."

"Children are terrible critics," I prosaically answered. "I'm really glad I haven't any."

"Do you also write, then? And in the same style as my brother? And do you like that style? And do people appreciate it in America? I don't write, but I think I feel." To these and various other inquiries and observations my young lady treated me till we heard her brother's step in the hall again and Mark Ambient reappeared. He was so flushed and grave that I supposed he had seen something symptomatic in the condition of his child. His sister apparently had another idea; she gazed at him from afar—as if he had been a burning ship on the horizon—and simply murmured "Poor old Mark!"

"I hope you're not anxious," I as promptly pronounced.

"No, but I'm disappointed. She won't let me in. She has locked the door, and I'm afraid to make a noise." I daresay there might have been a touch of the ridiculous in such a confession, but I liked my new friend so much that it took nothing for me from his dignity. "She tells me—from behind the door—that she'll let me know if he's worse."

"It's very good of her," said Miss Ambient with a hollow sound.

I had exchanged a glance with Mark in which it's possible he read that my pity for him was untinged with contempt, though I scarce know why he should have cared; and as his sister soon afterward got up and took her bedroom candlestick he proposed we should go back to his study. We sat there till after midnight; he put himself into his slippers and an old velvet jacket, he lighted an ancient pipe, but he talked considerably less than before. There were longish pauses in our communion, but they only made me feel we had advanced in intimacy. They helped me further to understand my friend's personal situation and to imagine it by no means the happiest possible. When his face was quiet it was vaguely troubled, showing, to my increase of interest—if that was all that was wanted!—that for him too life was the same struggle it had been for so many another man of genius. At last I prepared to leave him, and then, to my ineffable joy, he gave me some of the sheets of his forthcoming book—which, though unfinished, he had indulged in the luxury, so dear to writers of deliberation, of having "set up," from chapter to chapter, as he advanced. These early pages, the *prémices*, in the language of letters, of that new fruit of his imagination, I should take to my room and look over at my leisure. I was in the act of leaving him when the door of the study noiselessly opened and Mrs. Ambient stood before us. She observed us a moment, her candle in her hand, and then said to her husband that as she supposed he hadn't gone to bed she had come down to let him know Dolcino was more quiet and would probably be better in the morning. Mark Ambient made no reply; he simply slipped past her in the doorway, as if for fear she might seize him in his passage, and bounded upstairs to judge for himself of his child's condition. She looked so frankly discomfited that I for a moment believed her about to give him chase. But she resigned herself with a sigh and her eyes turned, ruefully and without a ray, to the lamplit room where various books at which I had been looking were pulled out of their places on the shelves and the fumes of tobacco hung in mid-air. I bade her good-night and then, without intention, by a kind of fatality, a perversity that had already made me address her overmuch on that question of her husband's powers, I alluded to the precious proof-sheets with which Ambient had entrusted me and which I nursed there under my arm. "They're the opening chapters of his new book," I said. "Fancy my satisfaction at being allowed to carry them to my room!"

She turned away, leaving me to take my candlestick from the table in the hall; but before we separated, thinking it apparently a good occasion to let me know once for all since I was beginning, it would seem, to be quite "thick" with my host—that there was no fitness in my appealing to her for sympathy in such a case; before we separated, I say, she remarked to me with her quick fine well-bred inveterate curtness: "I daresay you attribute to me ideas I haven't got. I don't take that sort of interest in my husband's proof-sheets. I consider his writings most objectionable!"

III

I HAD an odd colloquy the next morning with Miss Ambient, whom I found strolling in the garden before breakfast. The whole place looked as fresh and trim, amid the twitter of the birds, as if, an hour before, the housemaids had been turned into it with their dust-pans and feather-brushes. I almost hesitated to light a cigarette and was doubly startled when, in the act of doing so, I suddenly saw the sister of my host, who had, at the best, something of the weirdness of an apparition, stand before me. She might have been posing for her photograph. Her sad-coloured robe arranged itself in serpentine folds at her feet; her hands locked themselves listlessly together in front; her chin rested on a cinque-cento ruff. The first thing I did after bidding her good-morning was to ask her for news of her little nephew—to express the hope she had heard he was better. She was able to gratify this trust—she spoke as if we might expect to see him during the day. We walked through the shrubberies together and she gave me further light on her brother's household, which offered me an opportunity to repeat to her what his wife had so startled and distressed me with the night before. *Was* it the sorry truth that she thought his productions objectionable?

"She doesn't usually come out with that so soon!" Miss Ambient returned in answer to my breathlessness.

"Poor lady," I pleaded, "she saw I'm a fanatic."

"Yes, she won't like you for that. But you mustn't mind, if the rest of us like you! Beatrice thinks a work of art ought to have a 'purpose.' But she's a charming woman—don't you think her charming? I find in her quite the grand air."

"She's very beautiful," I produced with an effort; while I reflected that though it was apparently true that Mark Ambient was mismated it was also perceptible that his sister was perfidious. She assured me her brother and his wife had no other difference but this—one that she thought his writings immoral and his influence pernicious. It was a fixed idea; she was afraid of these things for the child. I answered that it was in all conscience enough, the trifle of a woman's regarding her husband's mind as a well of corruption, and she seemed much struck with the novelty of my remark. "But there hasn't been any of the sort of trouble that there so often is among married people," she said. "I suppose you can judge for yourself that Beatrice isn't at all—well, whatever they call it when a woman kicks over! And poor Mark doesn't make love to other people either. You might think he would, but I assure you he doesn't. All the same of course, from her point of view, you know, she has a dread of my brother's influence on the child on the formation of his character, his 'ideals,' poor little brat, his principles. It's as if it were a subtle poison or a contagion—something that would rub off on his tender sensibility when his father kisses him or holds him on his knee. If she could she'd prevent Mark from even so much as touching him. Every one knows it—visitors see it for themselves; so there's no harm in my telling you. Isn't it excessively odd? It comes from Beatrice's being so religious and so tremendously moral—so *à cheval* on fifty thousand *riguardi.* And then of course we mustn't forget," my companion added, a little unexpectedly, to this polyglot proposition, "that some of Mark's ideas are—well, really—rather impossible, don't you know?"

I reflected as we went into the house, where we found Ambient unfolding *The Observer* at the breakfast-table, that none of them were probably quite so "impossible, don't you know?" as his sister. Mrs. Ambient, a little "the worse," as was mentioned, for her ministrations, during the night, to Dolcino, didn't appear at breakfast. Her husband described her, however, as hoping to go to church. I afterwards learnt that she did go, but nothing naturally was less on the cards than that we should accompany her. It was while the church-bell droned near at hand that the author of "Beltraffio" led me forth for the ramble he had spoken of in his note. I shall attempt here no record of where we went or of what we saw. We kept to the fields and copses and commons, and breathed the same sweet air as the nibbling donkeys and the browsing sheep, whose woolliness seemed to me, in those early days of acquaintance with English objects, but part of the general texture of the small dense landscape, which looked as if the harvest were gathered by the shears and with all nature bleating and braying for the violence. Everything was full of expression for Mark Ambient's visitor—from the big bandy-legged geese whose whiteness was a "note" amid all the tones of green as they wandered beside a neat little oval pool, the foreground of a thatched and whitewashed inn, with a grassy approach and a pictorial sign—from these humble wayside animals to the crests of high woods which let a gable or a pinnacle peep here and there and looked even at a distance like trees of good company, conscious of an individual profile. I admired the hedge-rows, I plucked the faint-hued heather, and I was for ever stopping to say how charming I thought the thread-like footpaths across the fields, which wandered in a diagonal of finer grain from one smooth stile to another. Mark Ambient was abundantly good-natured and was as much struck, dear man, with some of my observations as I was with the literary allusions of the landscape. We sat and smoked on stiles, broaching paradoxes in the decent English air; we took short cuts across a park or two where the bracken was deep and my companion nodded to the old woman at the gate; we skirted rank coverts which rustled here and there as we passed, and we stretched ourselves at last on a heathery hillside where if the sun wasn't too hot neither was the earth too cold, and where the country lay beneath us in a rich blue mist. Of course I had already told him what I thought of his new novel, having the previous night read every word of the opening chapters before I went to bed.

"I'm not without hope of being able to make it decent enough," he said as I went back to the subject while we turned up our heels to the sky. "At least the people who dislike my stuff—and there are plenty of them, I believe—will dislike this thing (if it does turn out well) most." This was the first time I had heard him allude to the people who couldn't read him—a class so generally conceived to sit heavy on the consciousness of the man of letters. A being organised for literature as Mark Ambient was must certainly have had the normal proportion of sensitiveness, of irritability; the artistic *ego*, capable in some cases of such monstrous development, must have been in his composition sufficiently erect and active. I won't therefore go so far as to say that he never thought of his detractors or that he had any illusions with regard to the number of his admirers—he could never so far have deceived himself as to believe he was popular, but I at least then judged (and had occasion to be sure later on) that stupidity ruffled him visibly but little, that he had an air of thinking it quite natural he should leave many simple folk, tasting of him, as simple as ever he found them, and that he very seldom talked about the newspapers, which, by the way, were always even abnormally vulgar about him. Of course he may have thought them over—the newspapers—night and day; the only point I make is that he didn't show it while at the same time he didn't strike one as a man actively on his guard. I may add that, touching his hope of making the work on which he was then engaged the best of his books, it was only partly carried out. That place belongs incontestably to "Beltraffio," in spite of the beauty of certain parts of its successor. I quite believe, however, that he had at the moment of which I speak no sense of having declined; he was in love with his idea, which was indeed magnificent, and though for him, as I suppose for every sane artist, the act of execution had in it as much torment as joy, he saw his result grow like the crescent of the young moon and promise to fill the disk. "I want to be truer than I've ever been," he said, settling himself on his back with his hands clasped behind his head; "I want to give the impression of life itself. No, you may say what you will, I've always arranged things too much, always smoothed them down and rounded them off and tucked them in—done everything to them that life doesn't do. I've been a slave to the old superstitions."

"You a slave, my dear Mark Ambient? You've the freest imagination of our day!"

"All the more shame to me to have done some of the things I have! The reconciliation of the two women in 'Natalina,' for instance, which could never really have taken place. That sort of thing's ignoble—I blush when I think of it! This new affair must be a golden vessel, filled with the purest distillation of the actual; and oh how it worries me, the shaping of the vase, the hammering of the metal! I have to hammer it so fine, so smooth; I don't do more than an inch or two a day. And all the while I have to be so careful not to let a drop of the liquor escape! When I see the kind of things Life herself, the brazen hussy, does, I despair of ever catching her peculiar trick. She has an impudence, Life! If one risked a fiftieth part of the effects she risks! It takes ever so long to believe it. You don't know yet, my dear youth. It isn't till one has been watching her some forty years that one finds out half of what she's up to! Therefore one's earlier things must inevitably contain a mass of rot. And with what one sees, on one side, with its tongue in its cheek, defying one to be real enough, and on the other the *bonnes gens* rolling up their eyes at one's cynicism, the situation has elements of the ludicrous which the poor reproducer himself is doubtless in a position to appreciate better than any one else. Of course one mustn't worry about the *bonnes gens*," Mark Ambient went on while my thoughts reverted to his ladylike wife as interpreted by his remarkable sister.

"To sink your shaft deep and polish the plate through which people look into it—that's what your work consists of," I remember ingeniously observing.

"Ah polishing one's plate—that's the torment of execution!" he exclaimed, jerking himself up and sitting forward. "The effort to arrive at a surface, if you think anything of that decent sort necessary—some people don't, happily for them! My dear fellow, if you could see the surface I dream of as compared with the one with which I've to content myself. Life's really too short for art—one hasn't time to make one's shell ideally hard. Firm and bright, firm and bright is very well to say—the devilish thing has a way sometimes of being bright, and even of being hard, as mere tough frozen pudding is hard, without being firm. When I rap it with my knuckles it doesn't give the right sound. There are horrible sandy stretches where I've taken the wrong turn because I couldn't for the life of me find the right. If you knew what a dunce I am sometimes! Such things figure to me now base pimples and ulcers on the brow of beauty!"

"They're very bad, very bad," I said as gravely as I could.

"Very bad? They're the highest social offence I know; it ought—it absolutely ought; I'm quite serious—to be capital. If I knew I should be publicly thrashed else I'd manage to find the true word. The people who can't—some of them don't so much as know it when they see it—would shut their inkstands, and we shouldn't be deluged by this flood of rubbish!"

I shall not attempt to repeat everything that passed between us, nor to explain just how it was that, every moment I spent in his company, Mark

Ambient revealed to me more and more the consistency of his creative spirit, the spirit in him that felt all life as plastic material. I could but envy him the force of that passion, and it was at any rate through the receipt of this impression that by the time we returned I had gained the sense of intimacy with him that I have noted. Before we got up for the homeward stretch he alluded to his wife's having once—or perhaps more than once—asked him whether he should like Dolcino to read "Beltraffio." He must have been unaware at the moment of all that this conveyed to me—as well doubtless of my extreme curiosity to hear what he had replied. He had said how much he hoped Dolcino would read *all* his works—when he was twenty; he should like him to know what his father had done. Before twenty it would be useless; he wouldn't understand them.

"And meanwhile do you propose to hide them—to lock them up in a drawer?" Mrs. Ambient had proceeded.

"Oh no—we must simply tell him they're not intended for small boys. If you bring him up properly after that he won't touch them."

To this Mrs. Ambient had made answer that it might be very awkward when he was about fifteen, say; and I asked her husband if it were his opinion in general, then, that young people shouldn't read novels.

"Good ones—certainly not!" said my companion. I suppose I had had other views, for I remember saying that for myself I wasn't sure it was bad for them if the novels were "good" to the right intensity of goodness. "Bad for *them*, I don't say so much!" my companion returned. "But very bad, I'm afraid, for the poor dear old novel itself." That oblique accidental allusion to his wife's attitude was followed by a greater breadth of reference as we walked home. "The difference between us is simply the opposition between two distinct ways of looking at the world, which have never succeeded in getting on together, or in making any kind of common household, since the beginning of time. They've borne all sorts of names, and my wife would tell you it's the difference between Christian and Pagan. I may be a pagan, but I don't like the name; it sounds sectarian. She thinks me at any rate no better than an ancient Greek. It's the difference between making the most of life and making the least, so that you'll get another better one in some other time and place. Will it be a sin to make the most of that one, too, I wonder; and shall we have to be bribed off in the future state as well as in the present? Perhaps I care too much for beauty—I don't know, I doubt if a poor devil *can*; I delight in it, I adore it, I think of it continually, I try to produce it, to reproduce it. My wife holds that we shouldn't cultivate or enjoy it without extraordinary precautions and reserves. She's always afraid of it, always on her guard. I don't know what it can ever have done to her, what grudge it owes her or what resentment rides. And she's so pretty, too, herself! Don't you think she's lovely? She was at any rate when we married. At that time I wasn't aware of that difference I speak of—I thought it all came to the same thing: in the end, as they say. Well, perhaps it will in the end. I don't know what the end will be. Moreover, I care for seeing things as they are; that's the way I try to show them in any professed picture. But you mustn't talk to Mrs. Ambient about things as they are. She has a mortal dread of things as they are."

"She's afraid of them for Dolcino," I said: surprised a moment afterwards at being in a position—thanks to Miss Ambient—to be so explanatory; and surprised even now that Mark shouldn't have shown visibly that he wondered what the deuce I knew about it. But he didn't; he simply declared with a tenderness that touched me: "Ah nothing shall ever hurt *him*!"

He told me more about his wife before we arrived at the gate of home, and if he be judged to have aired overmuch his grievance I'm afraid I must admit that he had some of the foibles as well as the gifts of the artistic temperament; adding, however, instantly that hitherto, to the best of my belief, he had rarely let this particular cat out of the bag. "She thinks me immoral—that's the long and short of it," he said as we paused outside a moment and his hand rested on one of the bars of his gate; while his conscious expressive perceptive eyes—the eyes of a foreigner, I had begun to account them, much more than of the usual Englishman—viewing me now evidently as quite a familiar friend, took part in the declaration. "It's very strange when one thinks it all over, and there's a grand comicality in it that I should like to bring out. She's a very nice woman, extraordinarily well-behaved, upright and clever and with a tremendous lot of good sense about a good many matters. Yet her conception of a novel—she has explained it to me once or twice, and she doesn't do it badly as exposition—is a thing so false that it makes me blush. It's a thing so hollow, so dishonest, so lying, in which life is so blinked and blinded, so dodged and disfigured, that it makes my ears burn. It's two different ways of looking at the whole affair," he repeated, pushing open the gate. "And they're irreconcilable!" he added with a sigh. We went forward to the house, but on the walk, half-way to the door, he stopped and said to me: "If you're going into this kind of thing there's a fact you should know beforehand; it may save you some disappointment. There's a hatred of art, there's a hatred of literature—I mean of the genuine kinds. Oh the shams—those they'll swallow by the bucket!" I looked up at the charming house, with its genial colour and crookedness, and I answered with a smile that those evil passions might exist, but that I should never have expected to find them there. "Ah it doesn't matter after all," he a bit nervously laughed; which I was glad to hear, for I was reproaching myself with having worked him up.

If I had it soon passed off, for at luncheon he was delightful; strangely delightful considering that the difference between himself and his wife was, as he had said, irreconcilable. He had the art, by his manner, by his smile, by his natural amenity, of reducing the importance of it in the common concerns of life; and Mrs. Ambient, I must add, lent herself to this transaction with a very good grace. I watched her at table for further illustrations of that fixed idea of which Miss Ambient had spoken to me; for in the light of the united revelations of her sister-in-law and her husband she had come to seem to me almost a sinister personage. Yet the signs of a sombre fanaticism were not more immediately striking in her than before; it was only after a while that her air of incorruptible conformity, her tapering monosyllabic correctness, began to affect me as in themselves a cold thin flame. Certainly, at first, she resembled a woman with as few passions as possible; but if she had a passion at all it would indeed be that of Philistinism. She might have been (for there are guardian-spirits, I suppose, of all great principles) the very angel of the pink of propriety—putting the pink for a principle, though I'd rather put some dismal cold blue. Mark Ambient, apparently, ten years before, had simply and quite inevitably taken her for an angel, without asking himself of what. He had been right in calling my attention to her beauty. In looking for some explanation of his original surrender to her I saw more than before that she was, physically speaking, a wonderfully cultivated human plant—that he might well have owed her a brief poetic inspiration. It was impossible to be more propped and pencilled, more delicately tinted and petalled.

If I had had it in my heart to think my host a little of a hypocrite for appearing to forget at table everything he had said to me in our walk, I should instantly have cancelled such a judgement on reflecting that the good news his wife was able to give him about their little boy was ground enough for any optimistic reaction. It may have come partly, too, from a certain compunction at having breathed to me at all harshly on the cool fair lady who sat there—a desire to prove himself not after all so mismated. Dolcino continued to be much better, and it had been promised him he should come downstairs after his dinner. As soon as we had risen from our own meal Mark slipped away, evidently for the purpose of going to his child; and no sooner had I observed this than I became aware his wife had simultaneously vanished. It happened that Miss Ambient and I, both at the same moment, saw the tail of her dress whisk out of a doorway; an incident that led the young lady to smile at me as if I now knew all the secrets of the Ambients. I passed with her into the garden and we sat down on a dear old bench that rested against the west wall of the house. It was a perfect spot for the middle period of a Sunday in June, and its felicity seemed to come partly from an antique sun-dial which, rising in front of us and forming the centre of a small intricate parterre, measured the moments ever so slowly and made them safe for leisure and talk. The garden bloomed in the suffused afternoon, the tall beeches stood still for an example, and, behind and above us, a rose tree of many seasons, clinging to the faded grain of the brick, expressed the whole character of the scene in a familiar exquisite smell. It struck me as a place to offer genius every favour and sanction—not to bristle with challenges and checks. Miss Ambient asked me if I had enjoyed my walk with her brother and whether we had talked of many things.

"Well, of most things," I freely allowed, though I remembered we hadn't talked of Miss Ambient.

"And don't you think some of his theories are very peculiar?"

"Oh I guess I agree with them all." I was very particular, for Miss Ambient's entertainment, to guess.

"Do you think art's everything?" she put to me in a moment.

"In art, of course I do!"

"And do you think beauty's everything?"

"Everything's a big word, which I think we should use as little as possible. But how can we not want beauty?"

"Ah there you are!" she sighed, though I didn't quite know what she meant by it. "Of course it's difficult for a woman to judge how far to go," she went on. "I adore everything that gives a charm to life. I'm intensely sensitive to form. But sometimes I draw back—don't you see what I mean?—I don't quite see where I shall be landed. I only want to be quiet, after all," Miss Ambient continued as if she had long been baffled of this modest desire. "And one must be good, at any rate, must not one?" she pursued with a dubious quaver—an intimation apparently that what I might say one way or the other would settle it for her. It was difficult for me to be very original in reply, and I'm afraid I repaid her confidence with an unblushing platitude. I remember, moreover, attaching to it an inquiry, equally destitute of freshness and still more wanting perhaps in tact, as to whether she didn't mean to go to church, since that was an obvious way of being good. She made answer that she had performed this duty in the morning, and that for her, of Sunday afternoons, supreme virtue consisted in answering the week's letters. Then suddenly and without transition she brought out: "It's quite a mistake about Dolcino's being better. I've seen him and he's not at all right."

I wondered, and somehow I think I scarcely believed. "Surely his mother would know, wouldn't she?"

She appeared for a moment to be counting the leaves on one of the great beeches. "As regards most matters one can easily say what, in a given situation, my sister-in-law will, or would, do. But in the present case there are strange elements at work."

"Strange elements? Do you mean in the constitution of the child?"

"No, I mean in my sister-in-law's feelings."

"Elements of affection of course; elements of anxiety," I concurred. "But why do you call them strange?"

She repeated my words. "Elements of affection, elements of anxiety. She's very anxious."

Miss Ambient put me indescribably ill at ease; she almost scared me, and I wished she would go and write her letters. "His father will have seen him now," I said, "and if he's not satisfied he will send for the doctor."

"The doctor ought to have been here this morning," she promptly returned. "He lives only two miles away."

I reflected that all this was very possibly but a part of the general tragedy of Miss Ambient's view of things; yet I asked her why she hadn't urged that view on her sister-in-law. She answered me with a smile of extraordinary significance and observed that I must have very little idea of her "peculiar" relations with Beatrice; but I must do her the justice that she re-enforced this a little by the plea that any distinguishable alarm of Mark's was ground enough for a difference of his wife's. He was always nervous about the child, and as they were predestined by nature to take opposite views, the only thing for the mother was to cultivate a false optimism. In Mark's absence and that of his betrayed fear she would have been less easy. I remembered what he had said to me about their dealings with their son—that between them they'd probably put an end to him; but I didn't repeat this to Miss Ambient: the less so that just then her brother emerged from the house, carrying the boy in his arms. Close behind him moved his wife, grave and pale; the little sick face was turned over Ambient's shoulder and toward the mother. We rose to receive the group, and as they came near us Dolcino twisted himself about. His enchanting eyes showed me a smile of recognition, in which, for the moment, I should have taken a due degree of comfort. Miss Ambient, however, received another impression, and I make haste to say that her quick sensibility, which visibly went out to the child, argues that in spite of her affectations she might have been of some human use. "It won't do at all—it won't do at all," she said to me under her breath. "I shall speak to Mark about the Doctor."

Her small nephew was rather white, but the main difference I saw in him was that he was even more beautiful than the day before. He had been dressed in his festal garments—a velvet suit and a crimson sash—and he looked like a little invalid prince too young to know condescension and smiling familiarly on his subjects.

"Put him down, Mark, he's not a bit at his ease," Mrs. Ambient said.

"Should you like to stand on your feet, my boy?" his father asked.

He made a motion that quickly responded. "Oh yes; I'm remarkably well."

Mark placed him on the ground; he had shining pointed shoes with enormous bows. "Are you happy now, Mr. Ambient?"

"Oh yes, I'm particularly happy," Dolcino replied. But the words were scarce out of his mouth when his mother caught him up and, in a moment, holding him on her knees, took her place on the bench where Miss Ambient and I had been sitting. This young lady said something to her brother, in consequence of which the two wandered away into the garden together.

IV

I REMAINED with Mrs. Ambient, but as a servant had brought out a couple of chairs I wasn't obliged to seat myself beside her. Our conversation failed of ease, and I, for my part, felt there would be a shade of hypocrisy in my now trying to make myself agreeable to the partner of my friend's existence. I didn't dislike her—I rather admired her; but I was aware that I differed from her inexpressibly. Then I suspected, what I afterwards definitely knew and have already intimated, that the poor lady felt small taste for her husband's so undisguised disciple; and this of course was not encouraging. She thought me an obtrusive and designing, even perhaps a depraved, young man whom a perverse Providence had dropped upon their quiet lawn to flatter his worst tendencies. She did me the honour to say to Miss Ambient, who repeated the speech, that she didn't know when she had seen their companion take such a fancy to a visitor; and she measured apparently my evil influence by Mark's appreciation of my society. I had a consciousness, not oppressive but quite sufficient, of all this; though I must say that if it chilled my flow of small-talk it yet didn't prevent my thinking the beautiful mother and beautiful child, interlaced there against their background of roses, a picture such as I doubtless shouldn't soon see again. I was free, I supposed, to go into the house and write letters, to sit in the drawing-room, to repair to my own apartment and take a nap; but the only use I made of my freedom was to linger still in my chair and say to myself that the light hand of Sir Joshua might have painted Mark Ambient's wife and son. I found myself looking perpetually at the latter small mortal, who looked constantly back at me, and that was enough to detain me. With these vaguely-amused eyes he smiled, and I felt it an absolute impossibility to abandon a child with such an expression. His attention never strayed; it attached itself to my face as if among all the small incipient things of his nature throbbed a desire to say something to me. If I could have taken him on my own knee he perhaps would have managed to say it; but it would have been a critical matter to ask his mother to give him up, and it has remained a constant regret for me that on that strange Sunday afternoon I didn't even for a moment hold Dolcino in my arms. He had said he felt remarkably well and was especially happy; but though peace may have been with him as he pillowed his charming head on his mother's breast, dropping his little crimson silk legs from her lap, I somehow didn't think security was. He made no attempt to walk about; he was content to swing his legs softly and strike one as languid and angelic.

Mark returned to us with his sister; and Miss Ambient, repeating her mention of the claims of her correspondence, passed into the house. Mark came and stood in front of his wife, looking down at the child, who immediately took hold of his hand and kept it while he stayed. "I think Mackintosh ought to see him," he said; "I think I'll walk over and fetch him."

"That's Gwendolen's idea, I suppose," Mrs. Ambient replied very sweetly.

"It's not such an out-of-the-way idea when one's child's ill," he returned.

"I'm not ill, papa; I'm much better now," sounded in the boy's silver pipe.

"Is that the truth, or are you only saying it to be agreeable? You've a great idea of being agreeable, you know."

The child seemed to meditate on this distinction, this imputation, for a moment; then his exaggerated eyes, which had wandered, caught my own as I watched him. "Do *you* think me agreeable?" he inquired with the candour of his age and with a look that made his father turn round to me laughing and ask, without saying it, "Isn't he adorable?"

"Then why don't you hop about, if you feel so lusty?" Ambient went on while his son swung his hand.

"Because mamma's holding me close!"

"Oh yes; I know how mamma holds you when I come near!" cried Mark with a grimace at his wife.

She turned her charming eyes up to him without deprecation or concession. "You can go for Mackintosh if you like. I think myself it would be better. You ought to drive."

"She says that to get me away," he put to me with a gaiety that I thought a little false; after which he started for the Doctor's.

I remained there with Mrs. Ambient, though even our exchange of twaddle had run very thin. The boy's little fixed white face seemed, as before, to plead with me to stay, and after a while it produced still another effect, a very curious one, which I shall find it difficult to express. Of course I expose myself to the charge of an attempt to justify by a strained logic after the fact a step which may have been on my part but the fruit of a native want of discretion; and indeed the traceable consequences of that perversity were too lamentable to leave me any desire to trifle with the question. All I can say is that I acted in perfect good faith and that Dolcino's friendly little gaze gradually kindled the spark of my inspiration. What helped it to glow were the other influences—the silent suggestive garden-nook, the perfect opportunity (if it was not an opportunity for that it was an opportunity for nothing) and the plea I speak of, which issued from the child's eyes and seemed to make him say: "The mother who bore me and who presses me here to her bosom—sympathetic little organism that I am—has really the kind of sensibility she has been represented to you as lacking, if you only look for it patiently and respectfully. How is it conceivable she shouldn't have it? How is it possible that *I* should have so much of it—for I'm quite full of it, dear strange gentleman—if it weren't also in some degree in her? I'm my great father's child, but I'm also my beautiful mother's, and I'm sorry for the difference between them!" So it shaped itself before me, the vision of reconciling Mrs. Ambient with her husband, of putting an end to their ugly difference. The project was absurd of course, for had I not had his word for it—spoken with all the bitterness of experience—that the gulf dividing them was well-nigh bottomless? Nevertheless, a quarter of an hour after Mark had left us, I observed to my hostess that I couldn't get over what she had told me the night before about her thinking her husband's compositions "objectionable." I had been so very sorry to hear it, had thought of it constantly and wondered whether it mightn't be possible to make her change her mind. She gave me a great cold stare, meant apparently as an admonition to me to mind my business. I wish I had taken this mute counsel, but I didn't take it. I went on to remark that it seemed an immense pity so much that was interesting should be lost on her.

"Nothing's lost upon me," she said in a tone that didn't make the contradiction less. "I know they're very interesting."

"Don't you like papa's books?" Dolcino asked, addressing his mother but still looking at me. Then he added to me: "Won't you read them to me, American gentleman?"

"I'd rather tell you some stories of my own," I said. "I know some that are awfully good."

"When will you tell them? To-morrow?"

"To-morrow with pleasure, if that suits you."

His mother took this in silence. Her husband, during our walk, had asked me to remain another day; my promise to her son was an implication that I had consented, and it wasn't possible the news could please her. This ought doubtless to have made me more careful as to what I said next, but all I can plead is that it didn't. I soon mentioned that just after leaving her the evening before, and after hearing her apply to her husband's writings the epithet already quoted, I had on going up to my room sat down to the perusal of those sheets of his new book that he had been so good as to lend me. I had sat entranced till nearly three in the morning—I had read them twice over. "You say you haven't looked at them. I think it's such a pity you shouldn't. Do let me beg you to take them up. They're so very remarkable. I'm sure they'll convert you. They place him in—really—such a dazzling light. All that's best in him is there. I've no doubt it's a great liberty, my saying all this; but pardon me, and *do* read them!"

"Do read them, mamma!" the boy again sweetly shrilled. "Do read them!"

She bent her head and closed his lips with a kiss. "Of course I know he has worked immensely over them," she said; after which she made no remark, but attached her eyes thoughtfully to the ground. The tone of these last words was such as to leave me no spirit for further pressure, and after hinting at a fear that her husband mightn't have caught the Doctor I got up and took a turn about the grounds. When I came back ten minutes later she was still in her place watching her boy, who had fallen asleep in her lap. As I drew near she put her finger to her lips and a short time afterwards rose, holding him; it being now best, she said, that she should take him upstairs. I offered to carry him and opened my arms for the purpose; but she thanked me and turned away with the child still in her embrace, his head on her shoulder. "I'm very strong," was her last word as she passed into the house, her slim flexible figure bent backward with the filial weight. So I never laid a longing hand on Dolcino.

I betook myself to Ambient's study, delighted to have a quiet hour to look over his books by myself. The windows were open to the garden; the sunny stillness, the mild light of the English summer, filled the room without quite chasing away the rich dusky tone that was a part of its charm and that abode in the serried shelves where old morocco exhaled the fragrance of curious learning, as well as in the brighter intervals where prints and medals and miniatures were suspended on a surface of faded stuff. The place had both colour and quiet; I thought it a perfect room for work and went so far as to say to myself that, if it were mine to sit and scribble in, there was no knowing but I might learn to write as well as the author of "Beltraffio." This distinguished man still didn't reappear, and I rummaged freely among his treasures. At last I took down a book that detained me a while and seated myself in a fine old leather chair by the window to turn it over. I had been occupied in this way for half an hour—a good part of the afternoon had waned—when I became conscious of another presence in the room and, looking up from my quarto, saw that Mrs. Ambient, having pushed open the door quite again in the same noiseless way marking or disguising her entrance the night before, had advanced across the threshold. On seeing me she stopped; she had not, I think, expected to find me. But her hesitation was only of a moment; she came straight to her husband's writing-table as if she were looking for something. I got up and asked her if I could help her. She glanced about an instant and then put her hand upon a roll of papers which I recognised, as I had placed it on that spot at the early hour of my descent from my room.

"Is this the new book?" she asked, holding it up.

"The very sheets," I smiled; "with precious annotations."

"I mean to take your advice"—and she tucked the little bundle under her arm. I congratulated her cordially and ventured to make of my triumph, as I presumed to call it, a subject of pleasantry. But she was perfectly grave and turned away from me, as she had presented herself, without relaxing her rigour; after which I settled down to my quarto again with the reflexion that Mrs. Ambient was truly an eccentric. My triumph, too, suddenly seemed to me rather vain. A woman who couldn't unbend at a moment exquisitely indicated would never understand Mark Ambient. He came back to us at last in person, having brought the Doctor with him. "He was away from home," Mark said, "and I went after him to where he was supposed to be. He had left the place, and I followed him to two or three others, which accounts for my delay." He was now with Mrs. Ambient, looking at the child, and was to see Mark again before leaving the house. My host noticed at the end of two minutes that the proof-sheets of his new book had been removed from the table; and when I told him, in reply to his question as to what I knew about them, that Mrs. Ambient had carried them off to read he turned almost pale with surprise. "What has suddenly made her so curious?" he cried; and I was obliged to tell him that I was at the bottom of the mystery. I had had it on my conscience to assure her that she really ought to know of what her husband was capable. "Of what I'm capable? Elle ne s'en doute que trop!" said Ambient with a laugh; but he took my meddling very good-naturedly and contented himself with adding that he was really much afraid she would burn up the sheets, his emendations and all, of which latter he had no duplicate. The Doctor paid a long visit in the nursery, and before he came down I retired to my own quarters, where I remained till dinner-time. On entering the drawing-room at this hour I found Miss Ambient in possession, as she had been the evening before.

"I was right about Dolcino," she said, as soon as she saw me, with an air of triumph that struck me as the climax of perversity. "He's really very ill."

"Very ill! Why when I last saw him, at four o'clock, he was in fairly good form."

"There has been a change for the worse, very sudden and rapid, and when the Doctor got here he found diphtheritic symptoms. He ought to have been called, as I knew, in the morning, and the child oughtn't to have been brought into the garden."

"My dear lady, he was very happy there," I protested with horror.

"He would be very happy anywhere. I've no doubt he's very happy now, with his poor little temperature—!" She dropped her voice as her brother came in, and Mark let us know that as a matter of course Mrs. Ambient wouldn't appear. It was true the boy had developed diphtheritic symptoms, but he was quiet for the present and his mother earnestly watching him. She was a perfect nurse, Mark said, and Mackintosh would come back at ten. Our dinner wasn't very gay—with my host worried and absent; and his sister annoyed me by her constant tacit assumption, conveyed in the very way she nibbled her bread and sipped her wine, of having "told me so." I had had no disposition to deny anything she might have told me, and I couldn't see that her satisfaction in being justified by the event relieved her little nephew's condition. The truth is that, as the sequel was to prove, Miss Ambient had some of the qualities of the sibyl and had therefore perhaps a right to the sibylline contortions. Her brother was so preoccupied that I felt my presence an indiscretion and was sorry I had promised to remain over the morrow. I put it to Mark that clearly I had best leave them in the morning; to which he replied that, on the contrary, if he was to pass the next days in the fidgets my company would distract his attention. The fidgets had already begun for him, poor fellow; and as we sat in his study with our cigars after dinner he wandered to the door whenever he heard the sound of the Doctor's wheels. Miss Ambient, who shared this apartment with us, gave me at such moments significant glances; she had before rejoining us gone upstairs to ask about the child. His mother and his nurse gave a fair report, but Miss Ambient found his fever high and his symptoms very grave. The Doctor came at ten o'clock, and I went to bed after hearing from Mark that he saw no present cause for alarm. He had made every provision for the night and was to return early in the morning.

I quitted my room as eight struck the next day and when I came downstairs saw, through the open door of the house, Mrs. Ambient standing at the front gate of the grounds in colloquy with Mackintosh. She wore a white dressing-gown, but her shining hair was carefully tucked away in its net, and in the morning freshness, after a night of watching, she looked as much "the type of the lady" as her sister-in-law had described her. Her appearance, I suppose, ought to have reassured me; but I was still nervous and uneasy, so that I shrank from meeting her with the necessary challenge. None the less, however, was I impatient to learn how the new day found him; and as Mrs. Ambient hadn't seen me I passed into the grounds by a roundabout way and, stopping at a further gate, hailed the Doctor just as he was driving off. Mrs. Ambient had returned to the house before he got into his cart.

"Pardon me, but as a friend of the family I should like very much to hear about the little boy."

The stout sharp circumspect man looked at me from head to foot and then said: "I'm sorry to say I haven't seen him."

"Haven't seen him?"

"Mrs. Ambient came down to meet me as I alighted, and told me he was sleeping so soundly, after a restless night, that she didn't wish him disturbed. I assured her I wouldn't disturb him, but she said he was quite safe now and she could look after him herself."

"Thank you very much. Are you coming back?"

"No, sir; I'll be hanged if I come back!" cried the honest practitioner in high resentment. And the horse started as he settled beside his man.

I wandered back into the garden, and five minutes later Miss Ambient came forth from the house to greet me. She explained that breakfast wouldn't be served for some time and that she desired a moment herself with the Doctor. I let her know that the good vexed man had come and departed, and I repeated to her what he had told me about his dismissal. This made Miss Ambient very serious, very serious indeed, and she sank into a bench, with dilated eyes, hugging her elbows with crossed arms. She indulged in many strange signs, she confessed herself immensely distressed, and she finally told me what her own last news of her nephew had been. She had sat up very late—after me, after Mark—and before going to bed had knocked at the door of the child's room, opened to her by the nurse. This good woman had admitted her and she had found him quiet, but flushed and "unnatural," with his mother sitting by his bed. "She held his hand in one of hers," said Miss Ambient, "and in the other—what do you think?—the proof-sheets of Mark's new book!" She was reading them there intently: "did you ever hear of anything so extraordinary? Such a very odd time to be reading an author whom she never could abide!" In her agitation Miss Ambient was guilty of this vulgarism of speech, and I was so impressed by her narrative that only in recalling her words later did I notice the lapse. Mrs. Ambient had looked up from her reading with her finger on her lips—I recognised the gesture she had addressed me in the afternoon—and, though the nurse was about to go to rest, had not encouraged her sister-in-law to relieve her of any part of her vigil. But certainly at that time the boy's state was far from reassuring—his poor little breathing so painful; and what change could have taken place in him in those few hours that would justify Beatrice in denying Mackintosh access? This was the moral of Miss Ambient's anecdote, the moral for herself at least. The moral for me, rather, was that it *was* a very singular time for Mrs. Ambient to be going into a novelist she had never appreciated and who had simply happened to be recommended to her by a young American she disliked. I thought of her sitting there in the sick-chamber in the still hours of the night and after the nurse had left her, turning and turning those pages of genius and wrestling with their magical influence.

I must be sparing of the minor facts and the later emotions of this sojourn—it lasted but a few hours longer—and devote but three words to my subsequent relations with Ambient. They lasted five years—till his death—and were full of interest, of satisfaction and, I may add, of sadness. The main thing to be said of these years is that I had a secret from him which I guarded to the end. I believe he never suspected it, though of this I'm not absolutely sure. If he had so much as an inkling the line he had taken, the line of absolute negation of the matter to himself, shows an immense effort of the will. I may at last lay bare my secret, giving it for what it is worth; now that the main sufferer has gone, that he has begun to be alluded to as one of the famous early dead and that his wife has ceased to survive him; now, too, that Miss Ambient, whom I also saw at intervals during the time that followed, has, with her embroideries and her attitudes, her necromantic glances and strange intuitions, retired to a Sisterhood, where, as I am told, she is deeply immured and quite lost to the world.

Mark came in to breakfast after this lady and I had for some time been seated there. He shook hands with me in silence, kissed my companion, opened his letters and newspapers and pretended to drink his coffee. But I took these movements for mechanical and was little surprised when he suddenly pushed away everything that was before him and, with his head in his hands and his elbows on the table, sat staring strangely at the cloth.

"What's the matter, *caro fratello mio*?" Miss Ambient quavered, peeping from behind the urn.

He answered nothing, but got up with a certain violence and strode to the window. We rose to our feet, his relative and I, by a common impulse, exchanging a glance of some alarm; and he continued to stare into the garden. "In heaven's name what has got possession of Beatrice?" he cried at last, turning round on us a ravaged face. He looked from one of us to the other—the appeal was addressed to us alike.

Miss Ambient gave a shrug. "My poor Mark, Beatrice is always—Beatrice!"

"She has locked herself up with the boy—bolted and barred the door. She refuses to let me come near him!" he went on.

"She refused to let Mackintosh see him an hour ago!" Miss Ambient promptly returned.

"Refused to let Mackintosh see him? By heaven I'll smash in the door!" And Mark brought his fist down upon the sideboard, which he had now approached, so that all the breakfast-service rang.

I begged Miss Ambient to go up and try to have speech of her sister-in-law, and I drew Mark out into the garden. "You're exceedingly nervous, and Mrs. Ambient's probably right," I there undertook to plead. "Women know; women should be supreme in such a situation. Trust a mother—a devoted mother, my dear friend!" With such words as these I tried to soothe and comfort him, and, marvellous to relate, I succeeded, with the help of many cigarettes, in making him walk about the garden and talk, or suffer me at least to do so, for near an hour. When about that time had elapsed his sister reappeared, reaching us rapidly and with a convulsed face while she held her hand to her heart.

"Go for the Doctor, Mark—go for the Doctor this moment!"

"Is he dying? Has she killed him?" my poor friend cried, flinging away his cigarette.

"I don't know what she has done! But she's frightened, and now she wants the Doctor."

"He told me he'd be hanged if he came back!" I felt myself obliged to mention.

"Precisely—therefore Mark himself must go for him, and not a messenger. You must see him and tell him it's to save your child. The trap has been ordered—it's ready."

"To save him? I'll save him, please God!" Ambient cried, bounding with his great strides across the lawn.

As soon as he had gone I felt I ought to have volunteered in his place, and I said as much to Miss Ambient; but she checked me by grasping my arm while we heard the wheels of the dog-cart rattle away from the gate. "He's off—he's off—and now I can think! To get him away—while I think—while I think!"

"While you think of what, Miss Ambient?"

"Of the unspeakable thing that has happened under this roof!"

Her manner was habitually that of such a prophetess of ill that I at first allowed for some great extravagance. But I looked at her hard, and the next thing felt myself turn white. "Dolcino *is* dying then—he's dead?"

"It's too late to save him. His mother has let him die! I tell you that because you're sympathetic, because you've imagination," Miss Ambient was good enough to add, interrupting my expression of horror. "That's why you had the idea of making her read Mark's new book!"

"What has that to do with it? I don't understand you. Your accusation's monstrous."

"I see it all—I'm not stupid," she went on, heedless of my emphasis. "It was the book that finished her—it was that decided her!"

"Decided her? Do you mean she has murdered her child?" I demanded, trembling at my own words.

"She sacrificed him; she determined to do nothing to make him live. Why else did she lock herself in, why else did she turn away the Doctor? The book gave her a horror; she determined to rescue him—to prevent him from ever being touched. He had a crisis at two o'clock in the morning. I know that from the nurse, who had left her then, but whom, for a short time, she called back. The darling got munch worse, but she insisted on the nurse's going back to bed, and after that she was alone with him for hours."

I listened with a dread that stayed my credence, while she stood there with her tearless glare. "Do you pretend then she has no pity, that she's cruel and insane?"

"She held him in her arms, she pressed him to her breast, not to see him; but she gave him no remedies; she did nothing the Doctor ordered. Everything's there untouched. She has had the honesty not even to throw the drugs away!"

I dropped upon the nearest bench, overcome with my dismay—quite as much at Miss Ambient's horrible insistence and distinctness as at the monstrous meaning of her words. Yet they came amazingly straight, and if they did have a sense I saw myself too woefully figure in it. Had I been then a proximate cause—? "You're a very strange woman and you say incredible things," I could only reply.

She had one of her tragic headshakes. "You think it necessary to protest, but you're really quite ready to believe me. You've received an impression of my sister-in-law—you've guessed of what she's capable."

I don't feel bound to say what concession on this score I made to Miss Ambient, who went on to relate to me that within the last half-hour Beatrice had had a revulsion, that she was tremendously frightened at what she had done; that her fright itself betrayed her; and that she would now give heaven and earth to save the child. "Let us hope she will!" I said, looking at my watch and trying to time poor Ambient; whereupon my companion repeated all portentously "Let us hope so!" When I asked her if she herself could do nothing, and whether she oughtn't to be with her sister-in-law, she replied: "You had better go and judge! She's like a wounded tigress!"

I never saw Mrs. Ambient till six months after this, and therefore can't pretend to have verified the comparison. At the latter period she was again the type of the perfect lady. "She'll treat him better after this," I remember her sister-in-law's saying in response to some quick outburst, on my part, of compassion for her brother. Though I had been in the house but thirty-six hours this young lady had treated me with extraordinary confidence, and there was therefore a certain demand I might, as such an intimate, make of her. I extracted from her a pledge that she'd never say to her brother what she had just said to me, that she'd let him form his own theory of his wife's conduct. She agreed with me that there was misery enough in the house without her contributing a new anguish, and that Mrs. Ambient's proceedings might be explained, to her husband's mind, by the extravagance of a jealous devotion. Poor Mark came back with the Doctor much sooner than we could have hoped, but we knew five minutes afterwards that it was all too late. His sole, his adored little son was more exquisitely beautiful in death than he had been in life. Mrs. Ambient's grief was frantic; she lost her head and said strange things. As for Mark's—but I won't speak of that. *Basta, basta*, as he used to say.

Miss Ambient kept her secret—I've already had occasion to say that she had her good points—but it rankled in her conscience like a guilty participation and, I imagine, had something to do with her ultimately retiring from the world. And, apropos of consciences, the reader is now in a position to judge of my compunction for my effort to convert my cold hostess. I ought to mention that the death of her child in some degree converted her. When the new book came out (it was long delayed) she read it over as a whole, and her husband told me that during the few supreme weeks before her death—she failed rapidly after losing her son, sank into a consumption and faded away at Mentone—she even dipped into the black "Beltraffio."

About Author

Henry James OM (15 April 1843 – 28 February 1916) was an American-British author regarded as a key transitional figure between literary realism and literary modernism, and is considered by many to be among the greatest novelists in the English language. He was the son of Henry James Sr. and the brother of renowned philosopher and psychologist William James and diarist Alice James.

He is best known for a number of novels dealing with the social and marital interplay between émigré Americans, English people, and continental Europeans. Examples of such novels include The Portrait of a Lady, The Ambassadors, and The Wings of the Dove. His later works were increasingly experimental. In describing the internal states of mind and social dynamics of his characters, James often made use of a style in which ambiguous or contradictory motives and impressions were overlaid or juxtaposed in the discussion of a character's psyche. For their unique ambiguity, as well as for other aspects of their composition, his late works have been compared to impressionist painting.

His novella The Turn of the Screw has garnered a reputation as the most analysed and ambiguous ghost story in the English language and remains his most widely adapted work in other media. He also wrote a number of other highly regarded ghost stories and is considered one of the greatest masters of the field.

James published articles and books of criticism, travel, biography, autobiography, and plays. Born in the United States, James largely relocated to Europe as a young man and eventually settled in England, becoming a British subject in 1915, one year before his death. James was nominated for the Nobel Prize in Literature in 1911, 1912 and 1916.

Life

Early years, 1843–1883

James was born at 2 Washington Place in New York City on 15 April 1843. His parents were Mary Walsh and Henry James Sr. His father was intelligent and steadfastly congenial. He was a lecturer and philosopher who had inherited independent means from his father, an Albany banker and investor. Mary came from a wealthy family long settled in New York City. Her sister Katherine lived with her adult family for an extended period of time. Henry Jr. had three brothers, William, who was one year his senior, and younger brothers Wilkinson (Wilkie) and Robertson. His younger sister was Alice. Both of his parents were of Irish and Scottish descent.

The family first lived in Albany, at 70 N. Pearl St., and then moved to Fourteenth Street in New York City when James was still a young boy. His education was calculated by his father to expose him to many influences, primarily scientific and philosophical; it was described by Percy Lubbock, the editor of his selected letters, as "extraordinarily haphazard and promiscuous." James did not share the usual education in Latin and Greek classics. Between 1855 and 1860, the James' household traveled to London, Paris, Geneva, Boulogne-sur-Mer and Newport, Rhode Island, according to the father's current interests and publishing ventures, retreating to the United States when funds were low. Henry studied primarily with tutors and briefly attended schools while the family traveled in Europe. Their longest stays were in France, where Henry began to feel at home and became fluent in French. He was afflicted with a stutter, which seems to have manifested itself only when he spoke English; in French, he did not stutter.

In 1860 the family returned to Newport. There Henry became a friend of the painter John La Farge, who introduced him to French literature, and in particular, to Balzac. James later called Balzac his "greatest master," and said that he had learned more about the craft of fiction from him than from anyone else.

In the autumn of 1861 Henry received an injury, probably to his back, while fighting a fire. This injury, which resurfaced at times throughout his life, made him unfit for military service in the American Civil War.

In 1864 the James family moved to Boston, Massachusetts to be near William, who had enrolled first in the Lawrence Scientific School at Harvard and then in the medical school. In 1862 Henry attended Harvard Law School, but realised that he was not interested in studying law. He pursued his interest in literature and associated with authors and critics William Dean Howells and Charles Eliot Norton in Boston and Cambridge, formed lifelong friendships with Oliver Wendell Holmes Jr., the future Supreme Court Justice, and with James and Annie Fields, his first professional mentors.

His first published work was a review of a stage performance, "Miss Maggie Mitchell in Fanchon the Cricket," published in 1863. About a year later, A Tragedy of Error, his first short story, was published anonymously. James's first payment was for an appreciation of Sir Walter Scott's novels, written for the North American Review. He wrote fiction and non-fiction pieces for The Nation and Atlantic Monthly, where Fields was editor. In 1871 he published his first novel, Watch and Ward, in serial form in the Atlantic Monthly. The novel was later published in book form in 1878.

During a 14-month trip through Europe in 1869–70 he met Ruskin, Dickens, Matthew Arnold, William Morris, and George Eliot. Rome impressed him profoundly. "Here I am then in the Eternal City," he wrote to his brother William. "At last—for the first time—I live!" He attempted to support himself as a freelance writer in Rome, then secured a position as Paris correspondent for the New York Tribune, through the influence of its editor John Hay. When these efforts failed he returned to New York City. During 1874 and 1875 he published Transatlantic Sketches, A Passionate Pilgrim, and Roderick Hudson. During this early period in his career he was influenced by Nathaniel Hawthorne.

In 1869 he settled in London. There he established relationships with Macmillan and other publishers, who paid for serial installments that they would later publish in book form. The audience for these serialized novels was largely made up of middle-class women, and James struggled to fashion serious literary work within the strictures imposed by editors' and publishers' notions of what was suitable for young women to read. He lived in rented rooms but was able to join gentlemen's clubs that had libraries and where he could entertain male friends. He was introduced to English society by Henry Adams and Charles Milnes Gaskell, the latter introducing him to the Travellers' and the Reform Clubs.

In the fall of 1875 he moved to the Latin Quarter of Paris. Aside from two trips to America, he spent the next three decades—the rest of his life—in Europe. In Paris he met Zola, Alphonse Daudet, Maupassant, Turgenev, and others. He stayed in Paris only a year before moving to London.

In England he met the leading figures of politics and culture. He continued to be a prolific writer, producing The American (1877), The Europeans (1878), a revision of Watch and Ward (1878), French Poets and Novelists (1878), Hawthorne (1879), and several shorter works of fiction. In 1878 Daisy Miller established his fame on both sides of the Atlantic. It drew notice perhaps mostly because it depicted a woman whose behavior is outside the social norms of Europe. He also began his first masterpiece, The Portrait of a Lady, which would appear in 1881.

In 1877 he first visited Wenlock Abbey in Shropshire, home of his friend Charles Milnes Gaskell whom he had met through Henry Adams. He was much inspired by the darkly romantic Abbey and the surrounding countryside, which features in his essay Abbeys and Castles. In particular the gloomy monastic fishponds behind the Abbey are said to have inspired the lake in The Turn of the Screw.

While living in London, James continued to follow the careers of the "French realists", Émile Zola in particular. Their stylistic methods influenced his own work in the years to come. Hawthorne's influence on him faded during this period, replaced by George Eliot and Ivan Turgenev. 1879–1882 saw the publication of The Europeans, Washington Square, Confidence, and The Portrait of a Lady. He visited America in 1882–1883, then returned to London.

The period from 1881 to 1883 was marked by several losses. His mother died in 1881, followed by his father a few months later, and then by his brother Wilkie. Emerson, an old family friend, died in 1882. His friend Turgenev died in 1883.

Middle years, 1884–1897

In 1884 James made another visit to Paris. There he met again with Zola, Daudet, and Goncourt. He had been following the careers of the French "realist" or "naturalist" writers, and was increasingly influenced by them. In 1886, he published The Bostonians and The Princess Casamassima, both influenced by the French writers he'd studied assiduously. Critical reaction and sales were poor. He wrote to Howells that the books had hurt his career rather than helped because they had "reduced the desire, and demand, for my productions to zero". During this time he became friends with Robert Louis Stevenson, John Singer Sargent, Edmund Gosse, George du Maurier, Paul Bourget, and Constance Fenimore Woolson. His third novel from the 1880s was The Tragic Muse. Although he was following the precepts of Zola in his novels of the '80s, their tone and attitude are closer to the fiction of Alphonse Daudet. The lack of critical and financial success for his novels during this period led him to try writing for the theatre. (His dramatic works and his experiences with theatre are discussed below.)

In the last quarter of 1889, he started translating "for pure and copious lucre" Port Tarascon, the third volume of Alphonse Daudet adventures of Tartarin de Tarascon. Serialized in Harper's Monthly Magazine from June 1890, this translation praised as "clever" by The Spectator was published in January 1891 by Sampson Low, Marston, Searle & Rivington.

After the stage failure of Guy Domville in 1895, James was near despair and thoughts of death plagued him. The years spent on dramatic works were not entirely a loss. As he moved into the last phase of his career he found ways to adapt dramatic techniques into the novel form.

In the late 1880s and throughout the 1890s James made several trips through Europe. He spent a long stay in Italy in 1887. In that year the short novel The Aspern Papers and The Reverberator were published.

Late years, 1898–1916

In 1897–1898 he moved to Rye, Sussex, and wrote The Turn of the Screw. 1899–1900 saw the publication of The Awkward Age and The Sacred

Fount. During 1902–1904 he wrote The Ambassadors, The Wings of the Dove, and The Golden Bowl.

In 1904 he revisited America and lectured on Balzac. In 1906–1910 he published The American Scene and edited the "New York Edition", a 24-volume collection of his works. In 1910 his brother William died; Henry had just joined William from an unsuccessful search for relief in Europe on what then turned out to be his (Henry's) last visit to the United States (from summer 1910 to July 1911), and was near him, according to a letter he wrote, when he died.

In 1913 he wrote his autobiographies, A Small Boy and Others, and Notes of a Son and Brother. After the outbreak of the First World War in 1914 he did war work. In 1915 he became a British subject and was awarded the Order of Merit the following year. He died on 28 February 1916, in Chelsea, London. As he requested, his ashes were buried in Cambridge Cemetery in Massachusetts.

Biographers

James regularly rejected suggestions that he should marry, and after settling in London proclaimed himself "a bachelor". F. W. Dupee, in several volumes on the James family, originated the theory that he had been in love with his cousin Mary ("Minnie") Temple, but that a neurotic fear of sex kept him from admitting such affections: "James's invalidism ... was itself the symptom of some fear of or scruple against sexual love on his part." Dupee used an episode from James's memoir A Small Boy and Others, recounting a dream of a Napoleonic image in the Louvre, to exemplify James's romanticism about Europe, a Napoleonic fantasy into which he fled.

Dupee had not had access to the James family papers and worked principally from James's published memoir of his older brother, William, and the limited collection of letters edited by Percy Lubbock, heavily weighted toward James's last years. His account therefore moved directly from James's childhood, when he trailed after his older brother, to elderly invalidism. As more material became available to scholars, including the diaries of contemporaries and hundreds of affectionate and sometimes erotic letters written by James to younger men, the picture of neurotic celibacy gave way to a portrait of a closeted homosexual.

Between 1953 and 1972, Leon Edel authored a major five-volume biography of James, which accessed unpublished letters and documents after Edel gained the permission of James's family. Edel's portrayal of James included the suggestion he was celibate. It was a view first propounded by critic Saul Rosenzweig in 1943. In 1996 Sheldon M. Novick published Henry James: The Young Master, followed by Henry James: The Mature Master (2007). The first book "caused something of an uproar in Jamesian circles" as it challenged the previous received notion of celibacy, a once-familiar paradigm in biographies of homosexuals when direct evidence was non-existent. Novick also criticised Edel for following the discounted Freudian interpretation of homosexuality "as a kind of failure." The difference of opinion erupted in a series of exchanges between Edel and Novick which were published by the online magazine Slate, with the latter arguing that even the suggestion of celibacy went against James's own injunction "live!"—not "fantasize!"

A letter James wrote in old age to Hugh Walpole has been cited as an explicit statement of this. Walpole confessed to him of indulging in "high jinks", and James wrote a reply endorsing it: "We must know, as much as possible, in our beautiful art, yours & mine, what we are talking about — & the only way to know it is to have lived & loved & cursed & floundered & enjoyed & suffered — I don't think I regret a single 'excess' of my responsive youth".

The interpretation of James as living a less austere emotional life has been subsequently explored by other scholars. The often intense politics of Jamesian scholarship has also been the subject of studies. Author Colm Tóibín has said that Eve Kosofsky Sedgwick's Epistemology of the Closet made a landmark difference to Jamesian scholarship by arguing that he be read as a homosexual writer whose desire to keep his sexuality a secret shaped his layered style and dramatic artistry. According to Tóibín such a reading "removed James from the realm of dead white males who wrote about posh people. He became our contemporary."

James's letters to expatriate American sculptor Hendrik Christian Andersen have attracted particular attention. James met the 27-year-old Andersen in Rome in 1899, when James was 56, and wrote letters to Andersen that are intensely emotional: "I hold you, dearest boy, in my innermost love, & count on your feeling me—in every throb of your soul". In a letter of 6 May 1904, to his brother William, James referred to himself as "always your hopelessly celibate even though sexagenarian Henry". How accurate that description might have been is the subject of contention among James's biographers, but the letters to Andersen were occasionally quasi-erotic: "I put, my dear boy, my arm around you, & feel the pulsation, thereby, as it were, of our excellent future & your admirable endowment." To his homosexual friend Howard Sturgis, James could write: "I repeat, almost to indiscretion, that I could live with you. Meanwhile I can only try to live without you."

His numerous letters to the many young gay men among his close male friends are more forthcoming. In a letter to Howard Sturgis, following a long visit, James refers jocularly to their "happy little congress of two" and in letters to Hugh Walpole he pursues convoluted jokes and puns about their relationship, referring to himself as an elephant who "paws you oh so benevolently" and winds about Walpole his "well meaning old trunk". His letters to Walter Berry printed by the Black Sun Press have long been celebrated for their lightly veiled eroticism.

He corresponded in almost equally extravagant language with his many female friends, writing, for example, to fellow novelist Lucy Clifford: "Dearest Lucy! What shall I say? when I love you so very, very much, and see you nine times for once that I see Others! Therefore I think that—if you want it made clear to the meanest intelligence—I love you more than I love Others." To his New York friend Mary Cadwalader Jones: "Dearest Mary Cadwalader. I yearn over you, but I yearn in vain; & your long silence really breaks my heart, mystifies, depresses, almost alarms me, to the point even of making me wonder if poor unconscious & doting old Célimare [Jones's pet name for James] has 'done' anything, in some dark somnambulism of the spirit, which has ... given you a bad moment, or a wrong impression, or a 'colourable pretext' ... However these things may be, he loves you as tenderly as ever;

nothing, to the end of time, will ever detach him from you, & he remembers those Eleventh St. matutinal intimes hours, those telephonic matinées, as the most romantic of his life ..." His long friendship with American novelist Constance Fenimore Woolson, in whose house he lived for a number of weeks in Italy in 1887, and his shock and grief over her suicide in 1894, are discussed in detail in Edel's biography and play a central role in a study by Lyndall Gordon. (Edel conjectured that Woolson was in love with James and killed herself in part because of his coldness, but Woolson's biographers have objected to Edel's account.)

Works

Style and themes

James is one of the major figures of trans-Atlantic literature. His works frequently juxtapose characters from the Old World (Europe), embodying a feudal civilisation that is beautiful, often corrupt, and alluring, and from the New World (United States), where people are often brash, open, and assertive and embody the virtues—freedom and a more highly evolved moral character—of the new American society. James explores this clash of personalities and cultures, in stories of personal relationships in which power is exercised well or badly. His protagonists were often young American women facing oppression or abuse, and as his secretary Theodora Bosanquet remarked in her monograph Henry James at Work:

> When he walked out of the refuge of his study and into the world and looked around him, he saw a place of torment, where creatures of prey perpetually thrust their claws into the quivering flesh of doomed, defenseless children of light ... His novels are a repeated exposure of this wickedness, a reiterated and passionate plea for the fullest freedom of development, unimperiled by reckless and barbarous stupidity.

Critics have jokingly described three phases in the development of James's prose: "James I, James II, and The Old Pretender." He wrote short stories and plays. Finally, in his third and last period he returned to the long, serialised novel. Beginning in the second period, but most noticeably in the third, he increasingly abandoned direct statement in favour of frequent double negatives, and complex descriptive imagery. Single paragraphs began to run for page after page, in which an initial noun would be succeeded by pronouns surrounded by clouds of adjectives and prepositional clauses, far from their original referents, and verbs would be deferred and then preceded by a series of adverbs. The overall effect could be a vivid evocation of a scene as perceived by a sensitive observer. It has been debated whether this change of style was engendered by James's shifting from writing to dictating to a typist, a change made during the composition of What Maisie Knew.

In its intense focus on the consciousness of his major characters, James's later work foreshadows extensive developments in 20th century fiction. Indeed, he might have influenced stream-of-consciousness writers such as Virginia Woolf, who not only read some of his novels but also wrote essays about them. Both contemporary and modern readers have found the late style difficult and unnecessary; his friend Edith Wharton, who admired him greatly, said that there were passages in his work that were all but incomprehensible. James was harshly portrayed by H. G. Wells as a hippopotamus laboriously attempting to pick up a pea that had got into a corner of its cage. The "late James" style was ably parodied by Max Beerbohm in "The Mote in the Middle Distance".

More important for his work overall may have been his position as an expatriate, and in other ways an outsider, living in Europe. While he came from middle-class and provincial beginnings (seen from the perspective of European polite society) he worked very hard to gain access to all levels of society, and the settings of his fiction range from working class to aristocratic, and often describe the efforts of middle-class Americans to make their way in European capitals. He confessed he got some of his best story ideas from gossip at the dinner table or at country house weekends. He worked for a living, however, and lacked the experiences of select schools, university, and army service, the common bonds of masculine society. He was furthermore a man whose tastes and interests were, according to the prevailing standards of Victorian era Anglo-American culture, rather feminine, and who was shadowed by the cloud of prejudice that then and later accompanied suspicions of his homosexuality. Edmund Wilson famously compared James's objectivity to Shakespeare's:

One would be in a position to appreciate James better if one compared him with the dramatists of the seventeenth century—Racine and Molière, whom he resembles in form as well as in point of view, and even Shakespeare, when allowances are made for the most extreme differences in subject and form. These poets are not, like Dickens and Hardy, writers of melodrama—either humorous or pessimistic, nor secretaries of society like Balzac, nor prophets like Tolstoy: they are occupied simply with the presentation of conflicts of moral character, which they do not concern themselves about softening or averting. They do not indict society for these situations: they regard them as universal and inevitable. They do not even blame God for allowing them: they accept them as the conditions of life.

It is also possible to see many of James's stories as psychological thought-experiments. In his preface to the New York edition of The American he describes the development of the story in his mind as exactly such: the "situation" of an American, "some robust but insidiously beguiled and betrayed, some cruelly wronged, compatriot..." with the focus of the story being on the response of this wronged man. The Portrait of a Lady may be an experiment to see what happens when an idealistic young woman suddenly becomes very rich. In many of his tales, characters seem to exemplify alternative futures and possibilities, as most markedly in "The Jolly Corner", in which the protagonist and a ghost-doppelganger live alternative American and European lives; and in others, like The Ambassadors, an older James seems fondly to regard his own younger self facing a crucial moment.

Major novels

The first period of James's fiction, usually considered to have culminated in The Portrait of a Lady, concentrated on the contrast between Europe and America. The style of these novels is generally straightforward and, though personally characteristic, well within the norms of 19th-century fiction. Roderick Hudson (1875) is a Künstlerroman that traces the development of the title character, an extremely talented sculptor. Although the book shows some signs of immaturity—this was James's first serious attempt at a full-length novel—it has attracted favourable comment due to the vivid realisation of the three major characters: Roderick Hudson, superbly gifted but unstable and unreliable; Rowland Mallet, Roderick's limited but much more mature friend and patron; and Christina Light, one of James's most enchanting and maddening femmes fatales. The pair of Hudson and Mallet has been seen as representing the two sides of James's own nature: the wildly imaginative artist and the brooding conscientious mentor.

In The Portrait of a Lady (1881) James concluded the first phase of his career with a novel that remains his most popular piece of long fiction. The story is of a spirited young American woman, Isabel Archer, who "affronts her destiny" and finds it overwhelming. She inherits a large amount of money and subsequently becomes the victim of Machiavellian scheming by two American expatriates. The narrative is set mainly in Europe, especially in England and Italy. Generally regarded as the masterpiece of his early phase, The Portrait of a Lady is described as a psychological novel, exploring the minds of his characters, and almost a work of social science, exploring the differences between Europeans and Americans, the old and the new worlds.

The second period of James's career, which extends from the publication of The Portrait of a Lady through the end of the nineteenth century, features less popular novels including The Princess Casamassima, published serially in The Atlantic Monthly in 1885–1886, and The Bostonians, published serially in The Century Magazine during the same period. This period also featured James's celebrated Gothic novella, The Turn of the Screw.

The third period of James's career reached its most significant achievement in three novels published just around the start of the 20th century: The Wings of the Dove (1902), The Ambassadors (1903), and The Golden Bowl (1904). Critic F. O. Matthiessen called this "trilogy" James's major phase, and these novels have certainly received intense critical study. It was the second-written of the books, The Wings of the Dove (1902) that was the first published because it attracted no serialization. This novel tells the story of Milly Theale, an American heiress stricken with a serious disease, and her impact on the people around her. Some of these people befriend Milly with honourable motives, while others are more self-interested. James stated in his autobiographical books that Milly was based on Minny Temple, his beloved cousin who died at an early age of tuberculosis. He said that he attempted in the novel to wrap her memory in the "beauty and dignity of art".

Shorter narratives

James was particularly interested in what he called the "beautiful and blest nouvelle", or the longer form of short narrative. Still, he produced a number of very short stories in which he achieved notable compression of sometimes complex subjects. The following narratives are representative of James's achievement in the shorter forms of fiction.

- "A Tragedy of Error" (1864), short story
- "The Story of a Year" (1865), short story
- A Passionate Pilgrim (1871), novella
- Madame de Mauves (1874), novella
- Daisy Miller (1878), novella
- The Aspern Papers (1888), novella
- The Lesson of the Master (1888), novella
- The Pupil (1891), short story
- "The Figure in the Carpet" (1896), short story
- The Beast in the Jungle (1903), novella
- An International Episode (1878)
- Picture and Text
- Four Meetings (1885)
- A London Life, and Other Tales (1889)
- The Spoils of Poynton (1896)

- Embarrassments (1896)
- The Two Magics: The Turn of the Screw, Covering End (1898)
- A Little Tour of France (1900)
- The Sacred Fount (1901)
- Views and Reviews (1908)
- The Wings of the Dove, Volume I (1902)
- The Wings of the Dove, Volume II (1909)
- The Finer Grain (1910)
- The Outcry (1911)
- Lady Barbarina: The Siege of London, An International Episode and Other Tales (1922)
- The Birthplace (1922)

Plays

At several points in his career James wrote plays, beginning with one-act plays written for periodicals in 1869 and 1871 and a dramatisation of his popular novella Daisy Miller in 1882. From 1890 to 1892, having received a bequest that freed him from magazine publication, he made a strenuous effort to succeed on the London stage, writing a half-dozen plays of which only one, a dramatisation of his novel The American, was produced. This play was performed for several years by a touring repertory company and had a respectable run in London, but did not earn very much money for James. His other plays written at this time were not produced.

In 1893, however, he responded to a request from actor-manager George Alexander for a serious play for the opening of his renovated St. James's Theatre, and wrote a long drama, Guy Domville, which Alexander produced. There was a noisy uproar on the opening night, 5 January 1895, with hissing from the gallery when James took his bow after the final curtain, and the author was upset. The play received moderately good reviews and had a modest run of four weeks before being taken off to make way for Oscar Wilde's The Importance of Being Earnest, which Alexander thought would have better prospects for the coming season.

After the stresses and disappointment of these efforts James insisted that he would write no more for the theatre, but within weeks had agreed to write a curtain-raiser for Ellen Terry. This became the one-act "Summersoft", which he later rewrote into a short story, "Covering End", and then expanded into a full-length play, The High Bid, which had a brief run in London in 1907, when James made another concerted effort to write for the stage. He wrote three new plays, two of which were in production when the death of Edward VII on 6 May 1910 plunged London into mourning and theatres closed. Discouraged by failing health and the stresses of theatrical work, James did not renew his efforts in the theatre, but recycled his plays as successful novels. The Outcry was a best-seller in the United States when it was published in 1911. During the years 1890–1893 when he was most engaged with the theatre, James wrote a good deal of theatrical criticism and assisted Elizabeth Robins and others in translating and producing Henrik Ibsen for the first time in London.

Leon Edel argued in his psychoanalytic biography that James was traumatised by the opening night uproar that greeted Guy Domville, and that it plunged him into a prolonged depression. The successful later novels, in Edel's view, were the result of a kind of self-analysis, expressed in fiction, which partly freed him from his fears. Other biographers and scholars have not accepted this account, however; the more common view being that of F.O. Matthiessen, who wrote: "Instead of being crushed by the collapse of his hopes [for the theatre]... he felt a resurgence of new energy."

Non-fiction

Beyond his fiction, James was one of the more important literary critics in the history of the novel. In his classic essay The Art of Fiction (1884), he argued against rigid prescriptions on the novelist's choice of subject and method of treatment. He maintained that the widest possible freedom in content and approach would help ensure narrative fiction's continued vitality.

James wrote many valuable critical articles on other novelists; typical is his book-length study of Nathaniel Hawthorne, which has been the subject of critical debate. Richard Brodhead has suggested that the study was emblematic of James's struggle with Hawthorne's influence, and constituted an effort to place the elder writer "at a disadvantage." Gordon Fraser, meanwhile, has suggested that the study was part of a more commercial effort by James to introduce himself to British readers as Hawthorne's natural successor.

When James assembled the New York Edition of his fiction in his final years, he wrote a series of prefaces that subjected his own work to searching, occasionally harsh criticism.

At 22 James wrote The Noble School of Fiction for The Nation's first issue in 1865. He would write, in all, over 200 essays and book, art, and theatre reviews for the magazine.

For most of his life James harboured ambitions for success as a playwright. He converted his novel The American into a play that enjoyed modest returns in the early 1890s. In all he wrote about a dozen plays, most of which went unproduced. His costume drama Guy Domville failed disastrously on its opening night in 1895. James then largely abandoned his efforts to conquer the stage and returned to his fiction. In his Notebooks he maintained that his theatrical experiment benefited his novels and tales by helping him dramatise his characters' thoughts and emotions. James produced a small but valuable amount of theatrical criticism, including perceptive appreciations of Henrik Ibsen.

With his wide-ranging artistic interests, James occasionally wrote on the visual arts. Perhaps his most valuable contribution was his favourable assessment of fellow expatriate John Singer Sargent, a painter whose critical status has improved markedly in recent decades. James also wrote sometimes charming, sometimes brooding articles about various places he visited and lived in. His most famous books of travel writing include Italian Hours (an example of the charming approach) and The American Scene (most definitely on the brooding side).

James was one of the great letter-writers of any era. More than ten thousand of his personal letters are extant, and over three thousand have been published in a large number of collections. A complete edition of James's letters began publication in 2006, edited by Pierre Walker and Greg Zacharias. As of 2014, eight volumes have been published, covering the period from 1855 to 1880. James's correspondents included celebrated contemporaries like Robert Louis Stevenson, Edith Wharton and Joseph Conrad, along with many others in his wide circle of friends and acquaintances. The letters range from the "mere twaddle of graciousness" to serious discussions of artistic, social and personal issues.

Very late in life James began a series of autobiographical works: A Small Boy and Others, Notes of a Son and Brother, and the unfinished The Middle Years. These books portray the development of a classic observer who was passionately interested in artistic creation but was somewhat reticent about participating fully in the life around him.

Reception

Criticism, biographies and fictional treatments

James's work has remained steadily popular with the limited audience of educated readers to whom he spoke during his lifetime, and has remained firmly in the canon, but, after his death, some American critics, such as Van Wyck Brooks, expressed hostility towards James for his long expatriation and eventual naturalisation as a British subject. Other critics such as E. M. Forster complained about what they saw as James's squeamishness in the treatment of sex and other possibly controversial material, or dismissed his late style as difficult and obscure, relying heavily on extremely long sentences and excessively latinate language. Similarly Oscar Wilde criticised him for writing "fiction as if it were a painful duty". Vernon Parrington, composing a canon of American literature, condemned James for having cut himself off from America. Jorge Luis Borges wrote about him, "Despite the scruples and delicate complexities of James, his work suffers from a major defect: the absence of life." And Virginia Woolf, writing to Lytton Strachey, asked, "Please tell me what you find in Henry James. ... we have his works here, and

I read, and I can't find anything but faintly tinged rose water, urbane and sleek, but vulgar and pale as Walter Lamb. Is there really any sense in it?" The novelist W. Somerset Maugham wrote, "He did not know the English as an Englishman instinctively knows them and so his English characters never to my mind quite ring true," and argued "The great novelists, even in seclusion, have lived life passionately. Henry James was content to observe it from a window." Maugham nevertheless wrote, "The fact remains that those last novels of his, notwithstanding their unreality, make all other novels, except the very best, unreadable." Colm Tóibín observed that James "never really wrote about the English very well. His English characters don't work for me."

Despite these criticisms, James is now valued for his psychological and moral realism, his masterful creation of character, his low-key but playful humour, and his assured command of the language. In his 1983 book, The Novels of Henry James, Edward Wagenknecht offers an assessment that echoes Theodora Bosanquet's:

> "To be completely great," Henry James wrote in an early review, "a work of art must lift up the heart," and his own novels do this to an outstanding degree ... More than sixty years after his death, the great novelist who sometimes professed to have no opinions stands foursquare in the great Christian humanistic and democratic tradition. The men and women who, at the height of World War II, raided the secondhand shops for his out-of-print books knew what they were about. For no writer ever raised a braver banner to which all who love freedom might adhere.

William Dean Howells saw James as a representative of a new realist school of literary art which broke with the English romantic tradition epitomised by the works of Charles Dickens and William Makepeace Thackeray. Howells wrote that realism found "its chief exemplar in Mr. James... A novelist he is not, after the old fashion, or after any fashion but his own." F.R. Leavis championed Henry James as a novelist of "established pre-eminence" in The Great Tradition (1948), asserting that The Portrait of a Lady and The Bostonians were "the two most brilliant novels in the language." James is now prized as a master of point of view who moved literary fiction forward by insisting in showing, not telling, his stories to the reader. (Source: Wikipedia)

NOTABLE WORKS

NOVELS

Watch and Ward (1871)

Roderick Hudson (1875)

The American (1877)

The Europeans (1878)

Confidence (1879)

Washington Square (1880)

The Portrait of a Lady (1881)

The Bostonians (1886)

The Princess Casamassima (1886)

The Reverberator (1888)

The Tragic Muse (1890)

The Other House (1896)

The Spoils of Poynton (1897)

What Maisie Knew (1897)

The Awkward Age (1899)

The Sacred Fount (1901)

The Wings of the Dove (1902)

The Ambassadors (1903)

The Golden Bowl (1904)

The Whole Family (collaborative novel with eleven other authors, 1908)

The Outcry (1911)

The Ivory Tower (unfinished, published posthumously 1917)

The Sense of the Past (unfinished, published posthumously 1917)

SHORT STORIES AND NOVELLAS

A Tragedy of Error (1864)

The Story of a Year (1865)

A Landscape Painter (1866)

A Day of Days (1866)

My Friend Bingham (1867)

Poor Richard (1867)

The Story of a Masterpiece (1868)

A Most Extraordinary Case (1868)

A Problem (1868)

De Grey: A Romance (1868)

Osborne's Revenge (1868)

The Romance of Certain Old Clothes (1868)

A Light Man (1869)

Gabrielle de Bergerac (1869)

Travelling Companions (1870)

A Passionate Pilgrim (1871)

At Isella (1871)

Master Eustace (1871)

Guest's Confession (1872)

The Madonna of the Future (1873)

The Sweetheart of M. Briseux (1873)

The Last of the Valerii (1874)

Madame de Mauves (1874)

Adina (1874)

Professor Fargo (1874)

Eugene Pickering (1874)

Benvolio (1875)

Crawford's Consistency (1876)

The Ghostly Rental (1876)

Four Meetings (1877)

Rose-Agathe (1878, as Théodolinde)

Daisy Miller (1878)

Longstaff's Marriage (1878)

An International Episode (1878)

The Pension Beaurepas (1879)

A Diary of a Man of Fifty (1879)

A Bundle of Letters (1879)

The Point of View (1882)

The Siege of London (1883)

Impressions of a Cousin (1883)

Lady Barberina (1884)

Pandora (1884)

The Author of Beltraffio (1884)

Georgina's Reasons (1884)

A New England Winter (1884)

The Path of Duty (1884)

Mrs. Temperly (1887)

Louisa Pallant (1888)

The Aspern Papers (1888)

The Liar (1888)

The Modern Warning (1888, originally published as The Two Countries)

A London Life (1888)

The Patagonia (1888)

The Lesson of the Master (1888)

The Solution (1888)

The Pupil (1891)

Brooksmith (1891)

The Marriages (1891)

The Chaperon (1891)

Sir Edmund Orme (1891)

Nona Vincent (1892)

The Real Thing (1892)

The Private Life (1892)

Lord Beaupré (1892)

The Visits (1892)

Sir Dominick Ferrand (1892)

Greville Fane (1892)

Collaboration (1892)

Owen Wingrave (1892)

The Wheel of Time (1892)

The Middle Years (1893)

The Death of the Lion (1894)

The Coxon Fund (1894)

The Next Time (1895)

Glasses (1896)

The Altar of the Dead (1895)

The Figure in the Carpet (1896)

The Way It Came (1896, also published as The Friends of the Friends)

The Turn of the Screw (1898)

Covering End (1898)

In the Cage (1898)

John Delavoy (1898)

The Given Case (1898)

Europe (1899)

The Great Condition (1899)

The Real Right Thing (1899)

Paste (1899)

The Great Good Place (1900)

Maud-Evelyn (1900)

Miss Gunton of Poughkeepsie (1900)

The Tree of Knowledge (1900)

The Abasement of the Northmores (1900)

The Third Person (1900)

The Special Type (1900)

The Tone of Time (1900)

Broken Wings (1900)

The Two Faces (1900)

Mrs. Medwin (1901)

The Beldonald Holbein (1901)

The Story in It (1902)

Flickerbridge (1902)

The Birthplace (1903)

The Beast in the Jungle (1903)

The Papers (1903)

Fordham Castle (1904)

Julia Bride (1908)

The Jolly Corner (1908)

The Velvet Glove (1909)

Mora Montravers (1909)

Crapy Cornelia (1909)

The Bench of Desolation (1909)

A Round of Visits (1910)

OTHER

Transatlantic Sketches (1875)

French Poets and Novelists (1878)

Hawthorne (1879)

Portraits of Places (1883)

A Little Tour in France (1884)

Partial Portraits (1888)

Essays in London and Elsewhere (1893)

Picture and Text (1893)

Terminations (1893)

Theatricals (1894)

Theatricals: Second Series (1895)

Guy Domville (1895)

The Soft Side (1900)

William Wetmore Story and His Friends (1903)

The Better Sort (1903)

English Hours (1905)

The Question of our Speech; The Lesson of Balzac. Two Lectures (1905)

The American Scene (1907)

Views and Reviews (1908)

Italian Hours (1909)

A Small Boy and Others (1913)

Notes on Novelists (1914)

Notes of a Son and Brother (1914)

Within the Rim (1918)

Travelling Companions (1919)

Notebooks (various, published posthumously)

The Middle Years (unfinished, published posthumously 1917)

A Most Unholy Trade (1925, published posthumously)

The Art of the Novel : Critical Prefaces (1934)

CPSIA information can be obtained
at www.ICGtesting.com
Printed in the USA
LVHW091420011120
670391LV00003B/37

9 781662 715815